'Believe me, I've been ha— ever be playe— McGuire.'

She swallowed hard. 'please…'

'Please, what?'

'Just leave me alone.'

'No.'

'Oh, for goodness' sake!' Ally bit her lip and threw him a look that was half-impatient, half-desperate. 'There must be plenty of women out there who'd faint if you just smiled at them. Why not pick on one of them? Why me?'

'Why?' His eyes locked on hers. 'Because you're gutsy and beautiful and because you're fighting me every inch of the way.'

'Denting your ego, am I, Dr Nicholson?'

Sean threw back his head and laughed. 'Oh, no, Dr McGuire. My ego isn't that fragile.'

Sarah Morgan trained as a nurse and has since worked in a variety of health-related jobs. Married to a gorgeous businessman who still makes her knees knock, she spends most of her time trying to keep up with their two little boys, but manages to sneak off occasionally to indulge her passion for writing romance. Sarah loves outdoor life and is an enthusiastic skier and walker. Whatever she is doing, her head is always full of new characters and she is addicted to happy endings.

WORTH THE RISK

BY
SARAH MORGAN

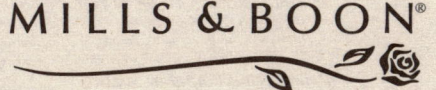

DID YOU PURCHASE THIS BOOK WITHOUT A COVER?
If you did, you should be aware it is **stolen property** as it was reported *unsold and destroyed* by a retailer. Neither the author nor the publisher has received any payment for this book.

All the characters in this book have no existence outside the imagination of the author, and have no relation whatsoever to anyone bearing the same name or names. They are not even distantly inspired by any individual known or unknown to the author, and all the incidents are pure invention.

All Rights Reserved including the right of reproduction in whole or in part in any form. This edition is published by arrangement with Harlequin Enterprises II B.V. The text of this publication or any part thereof may not be reproduced or transmitted in any form or by any means, electronic or mechanical, including photocopying, recording, storage in an information retrieval system, or otherwise, without the written permission of the publisher.

This book is sold subject to the condition that it shall not, by way of trade or otherwise, be lent, resold, hired out or otherwise circulated without the prior consent of the publisher in any form of binding or cover other than that in which it is published and without a similar condition including this condition being imposed on the subsequent purchaser.

MILLS & BOON and MILLS & BOON with the Rose Device are registered trademarks of the publisher.

First published in Great Britain 2000
Harlequin Mills & Boon Limited,
Eton House, 18-24 Paradise Road, Richmond, Surrey TW9 1SR

© Sarah Morgan 2000

ISBN 0 263 82286 9

Set in Times Roman 10 on 11¼ pt.
03-0101-54688

Printed and bound in Spain
by Litografia Rosés, S.A., Barcelona

CHAPTER ONE

ALLY was cold.

Last night, curled up with a hot chocolate in front of a cosy, flickering fire, a walk in the mountains had seemed like a good idea. Solitary. Invigorating. Good for the soul. Something she rarely had time for any more. The weather forecast had predicted a clear, fine day…

Tugging her hat further down over her ears to keep out the rising wind, she scowled at the swirling mist. How did the weatherman get away with it? If she ever got a diagnosis that wrong she'd be struck off!

With a resigned shrug she put her fingers in her mouth and gave a shrill whistle, bracing herself as a ball of fur streaked through the mist and skidded to a halt in front of her, tail wagging.

'This was a stupid idea!' She rammed her fingers back inside the glove before they froze, and glared at the dog. 'I don't know what you're looking so pleased about—I'm in the last stages of hypothermia. Let's call it a day.'

Dropping her hand to give him a quick pat, she turned on her heel and then stopped dead, every muscle in her body frozen into stillness. The dog growled.

'Did you hear something, too?' She listened again, straining her ears to pick out the sound again.

Nothing. Just the wind gusting more heavily by the minute.

Hesitation showing on her delicate features, Ally turned her head to gaze back up the path. It had come from the ghyll, a deep ravine plunging hundreds of feet down towards the valley floor.

Just the wind? Or a cry for help?

Her fingers tickled the dog's ears. 'It's probably nothing, but we'd better just check. We'll go higher up where the path is better.'

Down here the path was so badly eroded that going too close to the edge would be a quick route down to the bottom.

Her decision made, she turned on her heel and snapped her fingers at the dog, who fell into step behind her, tongue lolling. She stopped at the curve in the path and rubbed the dampness away from her face before dropping to her knees, inching as close to the vertiginous drop as she dared.

'Are you crazy?'

Hard male fingers bit into her shoulder and wrenched her back from the edge, leaving her spread-eagled on the stony path.

Her heart galloping with shock, Ally closed her eyes briefly and then opened them again to find herself staring at a pair of long, powerful legs. Blinking several times, her eyes moved slowly upwards, past broad shoulders, past a chunky polo-neck which brushed a rough jawline, and finally clashed with a pair of dark, very angry eyes.

Very angry indeed. With her?

Her heart still thumping, she scrambled to her feet, ignoring his outstretched hand. No way was she going to be on the receiving end of that grip twice in one day! The man obviously didn't know his own strength.

'What the hell were you doing?' His sharp question made her lift her chin defensively.

'What did you think I was doing?' Surely it was obvious?

'Contemplating suicide?'

'Oh, don't be ridiculous!' Ally gave him an impatient look and brushed some stones from her knees. 'I thought I heard someone shout.'

Smooth, dark eyebrows rose. 'So you thought you'd dive head first over the edge to investigate?'

'I wasn't anywhere near the edge—'

Strong fingers clamped around her wrist and jerked her back towards the head-spinning drop.

'See that?' He gestured with his head, a muscle working in his lean cheek as his eyes blazed into hers. 'This path is crumbling. You were seconds away from joining them at the bottom of the mountain.'

She tugged at her wrist. 'It's fine here. The National Trust have—' She broke off as his words registered. 'You said "them"! So you heard something, too?'

He gave a grim nod and released her, swinging a large rucksack off his back. 'There are two boys in trouble. They were scrambling in the ghyll.'

'Scrambling?' Ally's voice rang with disbelief. 'But we've had ten inches of rain in these fells since Monday. That ghyll is a difficult scramble at the best of times, but when it's been raining it's lethal. Were they roped up?'

He unclipped the top of his rucksack with gloved fingers, tugging the collar of his jacket higher to keep out the wind. 'They're just kids. I doubt they've even got a waterproof between them.'

'Oh, no!' Ally bit her lip and glanced anxiously towards the edge. 'We need to get help for them fast.'

'We do indeed.' He glanced up from the rucksack and studied her, those dark eyes sweeping every inch of her face and body before lingering on the logo of her quality weatherproof jacket.

She shifted uncomfortably. Something about those eyes made her feel suddenly gauche and tongue-tied. Like an eighteen-year-old student instead of a twenty-eight-year-old doctor with responsibilities. He had gorgeous eyes. Male eyes. Eyes you could stare into and lose yourself.

She blinked. 'We need to contact the mountain rescue team. I didn't bring a mobile phone.'

'I did, but there's no signal. I already tried.' He straightened and wiped a hand across his forehead. 'You and your party need to go down to the bottom and use a land-line.'

'And what will you do?'

He turned his attention back to the rucksack. 'Get down into that ravine and do what I can for them until help arrives.'

Ally stared at him. 'On your own?'

'You want me to take the sheep, too?'

Ally gritted her teeth. 'I'm suggesting that it might be wiser to wait for the mountain rescue team.'

'They'll take too long.' He delved into the rucksack and dragged out a coiled rope. 'The way those boys were equipped they'll die of hypothermia before you even make the phone call.'

Ally rubbed a hand over her numbed cheeks. The temperature was dropping fast. 'It's too dangerous. You can't climb down there on your own.'

'You have a better idea?'

She hadn't, not that he was exactly interested in her opinion anyway. He was too busy preparing for the descent into the ghyll, seemingly indifferent to the physical challenge it presented. Her heart missed a beat as he tugged off his hat and stuffed it into the top of his rucksack. He was heart-stoppingly handsome. Jet black hair cropped short and a firm mouth and jaw that was overwhelmingly male. For a moment Ally just stared. Then she shook herself and frowned instead. Why was she staring? She never stared at men. Never. Especially not handsome ones. They were bad news.

'I think what you're planning is really dangerous. How can you be so calm?'

'You'd prefer me to panic?'

The dry amusement in his tone made her flush slightly and she wrapped her arms around her body and looked at the threatening profile of the mountains. The weather was getting worse. Much worse.

'You're taking a huge risk.'

He rammed a helmet onto his head and glanced at the sky, assessing the weather. 'As long as the wind doesn't get any stronger it should be fine, although there's no way the RAF will be able to scramble a helicopter. If necessary we'll have to stretcher him off.'

Ally nodded. 'OK. Well, I'll wait until I know you're safely down—that way you can give me an idea of their condition before I contact the mountain rescue team.'

He gave a brief nod. 'That makes sense. Where are the rest of your party?'

Ally shifted slightly. 'I'm not in a party…'

There was an ominous silence. 'You're walking *alone*? In this weather?'

Her eyes avoided his. 'Yes, but I—'

'You crazy, irresponsible woman!' His gloved hand captured her chin and forced her to meet his incredulous gaze. 'You're walking on your own in the mountains in the middle of winter? You must be nuts!'

Her eyes flashed angrily and she jerked her chin away from his hand. 'Don't be a hypocrite! You're walking on your own, too, remember? And you're about to abseil down a rock on your own, so don't lecture me about safety!'

His jaw tightened. 'That's entirely different.'

Ally's chin lifted and her eyes clashed with his. 'Because you're a man and I'm a woman, I suppose?'

Anger blazed in his eyes and then suddenly faded and he gave her a sheepish smile that did strange things to her insides. 'Something like that.'

Ally swallowed hard. If he was handsome when he was angry then he was devastating when he smiled. The rapid transformation from macho condemnation to self-deprecating humour was as surprising as it was attractive.

She pulled herself together and glared at him. 'Has anyone ever told you you're a chauvinist?'

'Repeatedly.' His soft laugh warmed her insides. 'I just happen to think it isn't safe for a woman to be up in these mountains on her own. The weather is unpredictable and the world is full of perverts.'

'I'm equipped for bad weather and I have a dog to take care

of perverts.' Ally stamped her feet to keep warm and met his gaze squarely. 'So when you've finished indulging your prejudices perhaps we can finish working out a rescue plan.'

'I have worked out a rescue plan.' He hefted a rope, his mind obviously back on the job in hand. 'But I hadn't banked on you being on your own.'

'Why does that make a difference?'

'Because I was hoping for reinforcements, and one woman on her own is not reinforcements.'

Ally bristled defensively. 'What am I, then?'

'Frankly?' His mouth twisted into a wry smile. 'A liability.'

'A liability?' She gaped at him and he shrugged without a trace of apology.

'I don't need a dizzy blonde distracting me when I'm supposed to be concentrating. It's the same reason I don't believe women should be in the army. Men always have protective feelings towards them and that affects the job.'

Dizzy? Stunned into silence, Ally opened her mouth and closed it again. Her voice seemed to have given up the ghost. She tried again. 'Feel free to stifle your protective feelings. I don't need them.'

He shrugged. 'Well, like it or not, you've got them. And you're not going down this mountain on your own.'

She couldn't believe she was hearing this. 'I've been walking in these mountains on my own since my teens and I've never come to any harm.'

He glanced up, his eyes hard. 'Then you've been lucky. If you want to walk, join the Ramblers Association.'

'The Ramblers...' She broke off and her small chin lifted angrily. 'How dare you make judgements when you don't know anything about me? Dammit, you don't even know I'm blonde!'

His gaze lifted briefly to the wool hat, which successfully hid all traces of her hair colour and then rested on her face.

'I do know you're blonde.' His eyes smiled into hers for a

brief moment. 'I'm a connoisseur of blondes. Only true blondes have eyes the colour of violets.'

A connoisseur of blondes?

'And being a blonde makes me dizzy?' Her whole body was tingling with outrage and something else she chose not to identify. 'You are the most chauvinistic, misogynistic, prejudiced male—'

'And I like you, too.' He smiled complacently and then turned to look at the ravine, totally dismissive of her words, his mind obviously working on the problem ahead. How to evacuate the boys.

'Look.' She took a deep breath and deliberately made her tone conciliatory. 'I may be a woman but I do know these mountains and I can help—believe me.'

Judging from the look he gave her, he didn't. 'At a guess you're five feet nothing and eight stone. The chances of you being able to deploy any muscle to save those guys down there is remote.'

'Mountain rescue isn't about muscle.' Her fists clenched by her sides.

'No?' He tilted his head, his eyes hard. 'Didn't you say the water level is high at the moment? What if one of them has fallen into a dangerous position and needs to be moved to save his life? Good at lifting bulky teenagers, are you?'

Ally counted to ten. It wasn't enough so she tried twenty. 'Well, as you rightly said, someone needs to go for help, so once you give me a brief on their condition I'll alert mountain rescue.'

With a short laugh he turned his attention back to the rope. 'You're not going anywhere. The wind is getting worse, the path is barely visible and you're going down this mountain on your own over my dead body.'

Ally ground her teeth. The thought was actually quite attractive! 'I came up it on my own.'

'Ever heard the saying, "Two wrongs don't make a right"?'

He tugged off a glove to get a better grip on what he was doing.

Ally ignored his tone and scanned the items he'd laid on the ground. 'If you're really planning to abseil down to them this isn't the best place.'

He muttered something rude under his breath. 'You're trying to give me an abseiling lesson?'

'Yes.' She forced herself to hold his stare, refusing to be intimidated by his dry, forbidding tone. Obviously he thought she couldn't teach him anything, and his arrogance made her grind her teeth in frustration. Except that something told her that, however difficult the abseil, this man would manage it. He was supremely confident, very fit and, judging from the equipment he was pulling out of his rucksack, he obviously knew exactly what he was doing. But he didn't know the area like she did and it would be stupid to make the abseil more dangerous than it had to be.

'Do it from further up the gully. There's a six-metre waterfall directly beneath us and another one directly below that. It's a double cascade and totally unclimbable unless it's dry.'

He studied her in silence for a long moment, dark eyes narrowed. 'You're telling me you've abseiled into this ghyll?'

'Amazing, isn't it?' Her voice was honey-sweet. 'Even my blonde hair and blue eyes didn't hold me back.'

He stared at her. 'You're saying you can abseil?'

She batted her eyelashes in a parody of a dumb blonde. 'If I really concentrate hard I can even read and write.'

He grinned. 'OK, OK. So maybe I jumped to conclusions—'

'No, you?' Ally gave him a pert look, picked up the rope and slammed it against his chest. 'I know these mountains inside out and that ghyll is a death trap in weather like this. You need to be higher up. There are some flat rocks to the right of the falls. It's safer there and your rope is less likely to get snagged. And for your information, I'm five feet five, not five feet—above average for a woman, actually. I just seem smaller because you're tall. I weigh nine stone, and I may not have your volume of muscle but I'm extremely fit and more than capable of getting down this mountain in one piece and contacting the rescue services.'

Without waiting for his reply, she picked up his rucksack and trudged up the path, aware that he was close behind her.

'Do it from here.' She dumped his rucksack as far away from the edge as possible. 'There's a good place to anchor up there.'

He followed her gaze to a spiky rock above the path. 'Are you an only child?'

Ally blinked, totally thrown by his question. 'Sorry?'

'You must be,' he muttered under his breath, shaking his head and pulling a tape sling out of his rucksack.

'Why?' What was he talking about?

'Because, having had you, no mother would have the nerve to put herself through the worry again,' he said dryly. 'Your exploits must have given her heart failure. So you must be an only child. Or the youngest.'

Ally grinned in spite of herself. 'The youngest, actually. Shall I follow you down?'

'Have you got a helmet?'

'No.'

'Then you're staying here.' His eyes gleamed. 'Although, if you've spent your life being reckless, I don't suppose this is exactly the time to reform you. But as you rightly said, one of us needs to go for help. If you're sure you can do it without getting lost then that's the best solution.'

'Lost? Why should I get lost?' Ally held onto her temper. Just. 'Your opinion of women is appalling. Who on earth have you spent your life mixing with?'

'You want a list?' He gave her a wolfish grin and she could have bitten her tongue off. What a stupid thing to say. A man like him would have had women clawing each other to get at him since he could walk.

She changed the subject quickly, her voice crisp and businesslike. 'You do know not to move a casualty unless it's absolutely necessary?'

He raised an eyebrow. 'You'd like to add a first-aid lesson to your abseiling lesson?'

She flushed. 'I wasn't being rude. It's just that I'm a doctor and I thought that—'

'A doctor?' His eyes narrowed and she rolled her eyes.

'Don't tell me—you don't think women should be doctors.'

'Did I say that?'

He hadn't, of course, and, judging from the strange light in his eyes, she had a nasty feeling that he was overplaying the chauvinism just to wind her up. And she was falling for it every time...

'Just go and fetch the mountain rescue team and stop worrying.' This time his tone was gentle. 'I'm a doctor, too, so you can relax.'

Relax? He had to be kidding! She'd never be able to relax in his company in a million years! And he didn't look like any doctor she'd ever met. He looked more like someone from the SAS.

She watched while he checked the anchor point once more and adjusted his helmet, before looping a rope around his body in classic abseiling style.

'Ouch.' She wrinkled her nose. 'Not the most comfortable way of doing it.'

'You can say that again.' He gave her a rueful smile. 'Unfortunately, I didn't come out fully equipped for abseiling.'

'Will you be OK?'

'Oh, yes.' He gave a short laugh. 'My youth was as misspent as yours.'

'Well, be careful,' she mumbled. 'It's a difficult abseil.'

'I'll manage.' His eyes locked with hers. 'Are you sure you can get down the mountain safely? It goes against my better judgement to let you go alone...'

She smiled sweetly. 'Do us both a favour and leave your better judgement down there in the gully, will you?'

Why on earth did she find him so attractive? All he needed was a loincloth and he'd be the original Stone-Age man!

'Are you this prejudiced against all women or is it just blondes?'

He gave her a slow, sexy grin that melted her irritation faster than ice cream in a microwave. 'Don't misunderstand me, I've always been a sucker for blondes. In the right place.'

'And no doubt that's chained to the kitchen sink at home.'

'Barefoot and pregnant, you mean?' His eyes gleamed wickedly. 'Oh, no, sweetheart. If you were mine I wouldn't waste you in the kitchen.'

If she were his—

For a moment Ally stared into those dark eyes, seduced by the blatant interest she saw there, and then she shook herself. She wasn't his. She wasn't interested. She had Charlie now and they got on fine together. Life might not be exciting, but it was stable and predictable and that was what she wanted.

'Well, remind me to leave the bedroom window open so that you don't get stuck delivering the box of Milk Tray,' she snapped, determined not to show him how much he flustered her. His slow smile told her that her efforts were in vain. He knew all right.

'Humour me. Sending a woman down a mountain alone in this weather offends my notions of chivalry.' His eyes gleamed with appreciation. 'Even if she has got guts.'

'Well, chivalry isn't going to save those boys,' Ally pointed out briskly, pulling herself together rapidly and clicking her fingers at Hero, her dog, who bounded up eagerly. 'I'll wait while you abseil down.'

He gave a short nod and Ally tried not to look impressed as he went over the edge like a pro. There was no doubt that he knew what he was doing. He probably would have had heart failure if he'd seen the way she used to fling herself over the edge as a child. For several long minutes she hovered anxiously and then heard his voice, faint and muffled from deep down in the ghyll.

'I've got them. One of them has fractured his clavicle but he seems fine otherwise. The other is unconscious with a nasty head injury, fractured tibia and maybe a few broken ribs, judging from the way he's lying. Go as fast as you can but *be careful!*'

'Will do,' Ally yelled, whistling to the dog as she paced down the path as quickly as she felt was safe. Would she bring the team back in time?

It took two hours for her to return with the mountain rescue team and another hour for them to stretcher the two boys out of the ravine.

Ally's eyes widened as she recognised the first of the casualties, his arm secured in a broad sling.

'Andy? What on earth have you been doing?'

Despite his pallor, the boy coloured and looked thoroughly embarrassed.

'Look, we're really, really sorry, Dr McGuire…'

Ally made a soothing noise. Now wasn't the time to tell him off. 'Why weren't you roped up?'

Andy closed his eyes and shook his head, wincing with the pain. 'We didn't think we needed to. We judged it all wrong.'

'Well, you can say that again,' muttered Jack Morgan, leader of the mountain rescue team, who was co-ordinating the rescue. He threw an exasperated look in the direction of the injured youngster. 'Who's the other boy?'

Andy shifted on the stretcher. 'Pete. Pete Williams.'

'Oh, no! Not Pete!' Ally sprinted towards the edge of the ghyll to watch the second stretcher being lifted. She'd heard via the radio communications that the team had had trouble stabilising his injuries.

She'd known Pete for years. Ever since he'd first developed diabetes. Since then he'd devoted his short life to ignoring his diabetes and trying to prove he was no different from any other young teenager by getting into one scrape after another. And now he was seriously hurt. Her heart lurched and she mentally crossed her fingers as they lifted him up. Please, let him be OK. Please.

'He's in a bad way—we need the air support unit, really, but the weather's too foul. We'll have to carry him off.' Jack helped steady the second stretcher as they lowered it onto the hard ground. He glanced at the man who had masterminded the rescue from the bottom of the ghyll and did a double take.

'Nicholson?' Wide-mouthed with shock, he pushed his helmet back, a look of delight spreading across his craggy features. 'Damn, it is you! Sean, my boy, it's good to see you!'

Ally frowned and braced herself against a sudden gust of wind. The mist was clearing but the wind was rising steadily. 'You know him?'

Jack grinned. 'I do indeed. Not that I was expecting to see him. When you told me that some macho idiot had abseiled into the ghyll, I was expecting to find another crazy tourist.'

'Oh, thanks, Jack.' Ally closed her eyes briefly, flushing as she heard her less than complimentary description fed back to her and caught Sean's amused glance. Oh, well, at least he wasn't offended.

'So how are you, Sean?' Jack was oblivious to her embarrassment. 'What are you doing here?'

'Being in the wrong place at the wrong time as usual,' Sean muttered, wrenching off one of his gloves and checking the boy over again. 'I didn't know you were in charge of this lot now, Jack. This lad's in a bad way. Nasty head injury—in and out of consciousness—fractured ribs and a compound fracture of his tibia—we splinted that down below.'

'Right.' Jack frowned as he looked at the boy lying on the stretcher. 'Anything else?'

'He's wet through from the waterfall and heading for hypothermia. His right ankle's gone—but he was climbing in trainers so that's hardly surprising. At a guess that's probably why he slipped. We've put him in a polythene survival bag but we need to get a line in and get him off this mountain fast.'

'Trainers? In this weather?' Jack shook his head and exchanged a look with Sean. 'Nothing changes, does it? The mountains are still full of blithering idiots keeping us busy. Why on earth didn't he stay at home and watch television?'

'It's Wednesday. Nothing on.' Ted Wilson, the equipment officer, grinned wryly at his team-mates, his humour ever present even in an emergency.

Ally was on her knees beside the stretcher. 'Pete? Pete, can you hear me?'

The boy lay still, his pallor frightening.

'You know him?' Sean was frowning down at her and stupidly she felt tears prick her eyes. Poor, poor Pete.

'Yes.' She cleared her throat. 'He's one of my patients.'

'Local boys?' Jack rolled his eyes and shook his head, his look of exasperation tempered by the worry in his eyes. 'They should know better. It's bad enough rescuing tourists without having to start on the locals as well.'

Ally wanted to tell them that Pete was just trying to prove himself but she couldn't break a confidence so instead she mentioned the diabetes and then invested all her energy into doing what she could to save the boy. He groaned and opened his eyes, focusing with difficulty on the people around him.

'It's OK, Pete.' Ally ripped off one glove and stroked his face gently with her slim, warm fingers, before checking his pulse. At least he was conscious. 'You've hurt yourself, sweetheart, but we'll soon sort you out.'

'Big softy is our Ally. She ought to be reading him the riot act, not holding his hand,' Jack murmured to Sean, before picking up the radio and issuing more orders.

'S-sorry...' Pete winced and coughed slightly, his face contorting with pain.

Ally frowned. She didn't like the look of him one little bit. His lips were blue and his breathing was laboured and irregular. She glanced urgently up at Sean who was discussing the best way to carry the boys off the mountain.

'Problems?' In an instant he was crouched down next to her, the light-hearted banter of their previous encounter gone. The self-assurance was still there, but for some reason she found that oddly reassuring. She had a very bad feeling about young Pete.

'I can't—' Pete took a jerky breath and then another, and his eyes bulged with panic.

'It's OK, Pete. Just try and relax,' Ally soothed, jerking her head towards two of the team members who were hovering. 'Let's sit him up.'

Together they carefully lifted him into a sitting position so that he could breathe more easily and Ally looked at Sean. 'Pneumothorax?'

Sean nodded, his mouth a grim line. 'Could be. He's certainly broken some ribs.'

And one of those ribs could have punctured a lung.

'What's happening?' Jack was frowning and Sean rose to his feet in an easy movement, talking to Jack in low tones while Ally sat with Pete, monitoring his condition and reassuring him while he struggled with his breathing.

Gently she unzipped the top of his jacket and examined his neck, her heart sinking as she recognised the cardinal sign of pneumothorax. Giving Pete a quick smile, she stood up and joined Sean who was discussing the options with Jack.

She touched his arm, feeling the rock-hard muscle under his jacket. 'He's got tracheal deviation. We need to get him off this mountain fast.'

Sean shook his head, bracing himself against a sudden gust of wind. 'No way. It's compromising his breathing. If we could arrange an air evacuation then maybe we could risk leaving it, but as it is—' He broke off and gave a shrug. 'It's going to be a long and difficult carry off, and he's not going to make it unless we sort his breathing out.'

Jack frowned. 'So what do you suggest?'

'We'll have to put in a chest drain.' Sean gestured to the team members carrying the medical equipment.

'We carry a disposable chest drain,' Jack informed him quickly. 'It's just that we've never seen it used before.'

Sean gave a humourless laugh. 'Well, stick around—this is your lucky day.'

'What else do you need?' Jack was the epitome of professionalism, demonstrating with his quiet calm just how he'd managed to mastermind so many successful rescues over the years.

'Local anaesthetic and scalpel.'

Ally caught Sean's arm again, her expression urgent. 'Sean, you can't! It's too risky to put in a chest drain here.'

'You have a better suggestion?' Sean removed his thick protective gloves and flexed long, strong fingers.

'Not really.' Ally bit her lip and glanced anxiously at Pete, who was lying with his eyes closed, a bluish tinge surrounding his lips. 'But we're half way up a mountain—he might die…'

Sean moved her to one side and took some anaesthetic from one of the team. 'And if we do nothing he will almost certainly die. His breathing is becoming more compromised by the minute. Look at him.'

'But it's an emergency technique.'

Sean gave her a half-smile and unsheathed the needle. 'And this is an emergency.'

Ally watched him stride confidently over to Pete and tried to squash her anxiety. Maybe Sean was right. Maybe they had no choice.

She walked back to Pete and knelt beside him, smiling with a confidence she was far from feeling. Would Sean be able to do this?

'Leave him as much clothing as you can,' Sean ordered in an undertone. 'He's already colder than he should be.'

Carefully Ally removed Pete's jacket, watching Sean out of the corner of her eye as he snapped on sterile gloves.

'Jack, have you got strong scissors?'

They were slapped into her hand without question and as quickly as she could she cut through the fabric of Pete's jumper and shirt, exposing a small area of his ribs.

'Good thinking.' Sean was next to her, positioning himself

to give the local anaesthetic. 'He'll stay warmer that way. Jack, I need high-flow oxygen here.'

'On its way.' Jack handed the mask to Sean and hovered, watching over his shoulder. 'Do you want Entonox?'

Ally shook her head quickly and shifted to give Sean elbow room. 'No. Never in this sort of chest injury. It can turn a pneumothorax into a tension pneumothorax. What else have you got?'

'I'll look.' Jack vanished and returned in less than a minute with a syringe which he slapped into her rapidly freezing fingers. 'Any good?'

Ally scanned the label. 'Fine.'

'Tell us what you're doing, will you, Sean?' Jack stood behind Sean, squinting down at the younger man. 'We haven't seen this done before.'

Neither had Ally. At least, not since her casualty days years before, and never halfway up a mountain in a howling gale. She was a GP, for goodness' sake, not a trauma doctor. And what was Sean's specialty? He didn't seem at all nervous but, then, he didn't seem to be the sort of man who would ever be nervous about anything. His hands were rock steady and his manner totally relaxed, although Ally wasn't fooled. The man was working fast and with a skill that left her open-mouthed with awe.

'OK, he's had pain relief.' Ally handed the empty syringe to one of the team and flexed her fingers quickly to warm them. 'I'll get a line in while the anaesthetic works.'

Sean nodded approval and Ally reached out a hand for a venflon. Her fingers were stiff with cold and she seriously doubted she'd find a vein with Pete this cold. Still, maybe... She frowned down at his arm.

'Squeeze there for me, Jack.'

Jack's hands closed like a vice and she flicked the skin and mentally crossed her fingers. The cannula slid into the vein and she released her breath. Thank goodness.

Sean gave her a brief smile. 'Well done. Now get your

gloves back on before your hands freeze. OK, I've given local anaesthetic and I've prepared a sterile field. God, it's cold! I'm going to make a small incision here. You're doing well, Pete—this will help you breathe.'

Ally watched as he used the scalpel with quick precision and then inserted his gloved finger into the incision.

Jack hunkered down next to her, his voice soft. 'What's he doing that for?'

'To check that part of the lung isn't stuck to the chest wall,' Ally replied in an undertone, squeezing Pete's hand gently.

'That's fine,' Sean said quietly, and pushed the tube with just the required amount of force. 'I'm in. That should do it.'

Ally released the clamp.

'Cough for us, Pete,' Ally instructed gently, watching as air bubbled up through the fluid in the bottom of the drain.

'Bingo,' Sean muttered softly, rising to his feet in an easy movement and gesturing to Jack. 'That drain must be kept below the level of the lungs. If it goes any higher then the fluid drains back into his lungs and we're in trouble.'

Jack gave a brief nod, his expression grim. 'No problem. One of the lads can carry the drip and the other can carry the drain. Good work, Sean.'

Ally finished taping the drain securely and listened to Pete's chest, smiling with satisfaction at what she heard. Jack was right—Sean had done good work. And judging from his quiet confidence, he'd done the procedure many times before, but surely not in circumstances as difficult as these?

He caught her glance and raised an eyebrow. 'What?'

Her eyes teased him with a mixture of humour and admiration. 'I don't know what sort of doctor you are but I'd hazard a guess that you're not an obstetrician.'

'You don't think I can deliver a baby?'

Ally had to admit that the man would probably succeed at anything he set his hand to. 'Well, that was pretty impressive, Dr Nicholson.'

'For a macho idiot, you mean?' His teasing drawl made her blush.

'I admit that my first impression of you was wrong—but you called me a dizzy blonde.'

'So I did.' His smile faded and his gaze was intent. 'And I was wrong about that, too, wasn't I? So maybe we're quits.'

Ally shifted under his watchful scrutiny, suddenly aware of every female part of herself. She'd never met a man who made her feel more like a woman than Sean did. To cover her awkwardness she concentrated on making Pete comfortable, aware that Sean was still watching her while the mountain rescue team made the final preparations for their descent.

'You made good time down that mountain. The mist was awful—I thought you might get lost.'

Jack glanced curiously from one to the other and gave a short laugh. 'Lost? Our Ally? You have to be kidding! She used to be our best team member until—'

'We're ready when you are, Jack,' Ally interrupted quickly, reluctant to have the details of her private life broadcast to this stranger.

Sean gave her a sharp look. 'You were in the mountain rescue team?'

Ally's eyes challenged him. 'They do take blondes, you know.'

Sean's eyes gleamed with appreciation but he carried on dealing with the patient, skilfully preparing him for the arduous trip down the mountain.

Jack snorted. 'Ally was in the team for more than a while. She knows these fells like you know the inside of a beer can. She wouldn't get lost if you put her head in a bag.'

'Now, there's an idea for keeping her quiet,' Sean said dryly, tugging on his gloves and yanking his Balaclava back down over his face. 'OK, folks, let's get these guys off this mountain.'

CHAPTER TWO

IT TOOK the best part of an hour before they reached the waiting ambulance. Ally and Sean supervised as the stretchers were lifted into the vehicles.

Risking a surreptitious glance at Sean, Ally's eyes skimmed his hard, male profile, resting for a moment on the strong nose and dark jaw.

'Good-looking devil, isn't he?' Jack shot her a knowing grin and she gave him what she hoped was a casual smile as they moved away from the ambulance.

'If you like Milk Tray.'

Jack looked baffled. 'What's Milk Tray got to do with it?'

Ally's cheeks dimpled into an impish grin. 'You know, man dives under water, scales mountains, leaps off cliffs and all because the lady loves…remember?'

Jack grinned. 'Oh, right. Yes, that's our Sean. Women usually can't leave him alone.'

She could well believe it. There surely wasn't a woman alive who wouldn't find Sean Nicholson attractive. Dark-fringed lashes shielded an expression of cool indifference which she'd seen change to burning anger and molten sexuality.

As if sensing her scrutiny, he turned suddenly, one dark eyebrow lifting questioningly as he caught her looking at him. Throwing a final remark to one of the team members, he strode over to them, his eyes fixed on Ally.

'Take a hike, Jack.' It was a quiet order and Jack glanced curiously at the two of them before strolling back to his colleagues, whistling softly.

Ally's heart thudded. Why on earth had she been stupid enough to get caught staring like a besotted teenager?

'So how do you know Jack?' She huddled deeper inside her

jacket, although whether for protection from the weather or Sean she wasn't sure. He made her nervous and he knew it.

'I don't want to talk about Jack.'

Ally shrugged casually and concentrated on watching the ambulance. 'So what do you want to talk about, Dr Nicholson?'

'Us.'

Her heart stumbled and her eyes flew to his. 'Us?'

He reached out a hand and tugged off her hat, a wry smile twisting his firm mouth as her totally unmanageable blonde curls tumbled over her shoulders.

'So…I was half right. Blonde—but not dizzy.'

Ally took a deep breath. She was feeling pretty dizzy at that precise moment.

'Sean—'

'I want to see you again, Ally.'

His eyes trapped hers and her heart thudded against her ribcage. The man certainly came straight to the point. Whatever happened to 'perhaps you might like to' or 'would you consider?'. But that was Sean all over, or so it seemed. What the man wanted, the man got.

She lifted her chin and feigned indifference. 'Why? You want abseiling lessons or first-aid training?' She used bravado to cover up how shy and uncomfortable this man made her feel, and he laughed out loud, a powerful figure, his feet planted slightly apart, shielding her from the curious glances of the rest of the mountain rescue team.

'Neither.' His smile curled around her insides. 'I want you, Dr McGuire.'

Her palms were damp and her breathing was difficult. 'And what about what I want, Dr Nicholson?'

His lazy, totally male appraisal made her heart lurch. 'You want exactly the same as me—it's just a question of whether you're brave enough to admit it on such short acquaintance.'

For a moment Ally stared at him, almost hypnotised by his gaze. She didn't want the same as him. She didn't. She had

Charlie. A safe, steady relationship with none of the fire and heat that this man poured over her.

'You're assuming I'm not involved with anyone.'

He stared at her for a long moment, a muscle working in that hard jaw. 'Are you?'

'Yes.'

'And he lets you wander the fells on your own?' He scowled angrily. 'You should ditch him. No man worth his salt would allow that. He should be protecting you.'

'Charlie doesn't own me.' She forced herself to hold his gaze. 'And I don't need protecting.'

His jaw tightened. 'That's a matter of opinion.'

'Sean, we're off!!' Jack shouted across to them, and Sean's mouth tightened.

'We'll finish this discussion another time.'

He turned on his heel and walked towards the ambulance, leaving her trembling. What did he mean, they'd finish the discussion another time? With shaking hands she pulled her hat on. She didn't want there to be another time. She never, ever wanted to see him again. Not if she lived to be a hundred. He made her feel vulnerable and exposed. He brought all her emotions to the surface, emotions that had been hidden for a long time and needed to stay hidden. She didn't want to be forced to confront those feelings. She had Charlie now, and life might not be exciting but it was stable and predictable and that was all she wanted. Wasn't it?

'Mummy, did you really save two boys?'

'Who told you that?' Ally sipped her tea and mentally ran through everything she had to do before surgery. Mornings were always such a rush.

'Uncle Jack.' The little girl pushed her arm into the cereal packet and removed a fistful of cornflakes.

'Charlotte McGuire, that's disgusting!' Ally removed the packet with a frown and pushed a piece of toast towards her daughter. 'If you're still hungry eat some toast.'

Blue eyes clashed with hers. 'Toast is yuck.'

Ally took a deep breath, reminding herself that mealtimes should never be a battleground. 'You liked toast yesterday.'

'Well, I hate it today.' Charlie scowled and then shrugged, obviously deciding that the toast looked quite tempting. 'OK. One piece. If you shape it like a house. Why didn't they die?'

Calmly Ally buttered the toast and cut out windows and a door. 'Why didn't who die?'

'Those boys.' Charlie munched happily, obviously forgetting that toast was supposed to be 'yuck'. 'Uncle Jack told Grandma that they were lucky you happened to be there because if you hadn't they might have died.'

'Well, they certainly shouldn't have been walking without the right equipment.' Making a mental note to talk to Jack about being so graphic in front of five-year-olds, Ally picked up the rest of the breakfast things and stacked them in the sink.

'How would they have died?'

Ally gritted her teeth. Thanks, Jack. Thanks a bunch. 'Well, it was very cold, sweetheart, and people can die of being too cold. But they're fine now, so why don't you just forget about them and get ready for school?'

Charlie didn't want to forget it. 'Karen doesn't always wear her coat in the playground so does that mean she could die?'

'No, it doesn't,' Ally said quickly, wiping her hands on the towel. 'It isn't the same thing at all. The boys on the mountain were wet through from a waterfall and that made them even colder. And up in the mountains is much colder than the playground. Now then, if you don't hurry up and clean your teeth you're going to be late.'

Charlie slipped off the stool, skipping through the kitchen to the stairs.

Ally breathed a sigh of relief. Having a five-year-old with an enquiring mind was a mixed blessing.

She grabbed both coats and Charlie's schoolbag, and they climbed into Ally's little car to drive the short distance to her friend Karen's house.

They were met at the door by Tina, Karen's mother.

'Hi, there!' She gave them a bright smile and ruffled Charlie's hair as the little girl darted past her to join her friend who was finishing breakfast in the kitchen.

Ally bit her lip and looked at her gratefully. 'Thanks, Tina. I don't know what I'd do without—'

'Forget it! You know we love having her.' Tina gave her a friendly push. 'Get going or you'll be late for surgery. Don't forget our Hallowe'en party on Saturday. Are you coming?'

Ally shook her head. 'I'm working, but Mum will bring her.'

She gave her friend a quick hug and sprinted back to her car, thinking how fortunate she was to have a good friend who was prepared to have Charlie to play every morning for the short time before school so that she herself was able to make morning surgery without being late. Her parents collected Charlie after school and looked after her until Ally finished evening surgery. Fortunately the senior partner, Will Carter, restricted her on-call responsibilities so she rarely worked evenings or weekends. All in all, the arrangements worked well, although she would have liked to be at home for Charlie more.

A feeling of sadness shot through her and she pushed it away. She had no choice about the way things were and she never had. She did the best she could in the circumstances.

She pulled into the surgery at the same time as Will.

'Morning, beautiful! How's that girl of yours?'

Ally rolled her eyes. 'Too inquisitive for her own good.'

Will laughed. 'You wait. It gets worse.'

'Don't tell me that!' Ally threw him a grin. She adored Will. Nearing retirement age, he had developed a practice that the whole of Cumbria admired. Without Will she would never have survived the trauma that had surrounded Charlie's arrival. 'Karen Butler is having a Hallowe'en party on Saturday and they're all dying of excitement.'

Will frowned and pushed open the health centre door for her. 'Aren't you working on Saturday?'

'Yes, but it's not a problem.' Ally tucked a strand of blonde hair behind her ear. 'My mum is taking her and that's fine by Charlie.'

'Sure?'

Ally nodded as they walked through to the spacious reception area. 'Quite sure, Will, but thanks for the thought.'

She knew that Will would have taken over at the drop of a hat and she didn't want that happening. He already picked up more than enough of her workload so that she could spend as much time as possible with Charlie.

Will greeted the reception staff in his usual cheery manner and strode through to the staffroom, still talking to Ally.

'Talking about Saturday, Tony Masters is having a dinner party and I thought—'

'The answer's no, Will!' Ally interrupted immediately, knowing what was coming. The same thing that happened every time they were on their own together. Will trying to play Cupid. With the best of intentions, admittedly. 'I know what you're going to say, and not only do I hate dinner parties where I'm the available woman but I'm quite happy as I am. I don't need you matchmaking.'

Will scowled and flicked the switch on the kettle. 'Ally, you're young and beautiful and you shouldn't bury yourself because of Charlie.'

'Charlie and I are fine.' Ally shrugged off her coat and hung it up, before filling her mug and standing by the door ready to make her escape into her consulting room.

Will's mouth tightened. 'You're far from fine! You don't have a social life, apart from Charlie's friends, I know you struggle financially because that louse—'

'I'm independent, Will, and that's what matters to me.' Ally gave him a gentle smile. 'It's love and constancy that matter to a child, not luxuries. Charlie and I are happy. You're much more upset about it than I am!'

'Too right I'm upset about it,' Will growled. 'You should have someone to look after you.'

'Oh, yes?' Ally's gentle blue eyes hardened. 'Well, the men

I meet aren't very good at that if you remember, so now I look after both of us by myself. On my own.'

Will looked sad. 'You deserve so much more...'

Ally's face softened and on impulse she walked over to him and gave him a kiss on the cheek. 'You're a lovely man, Will, but there aren't too many like you around.'

Will stared down at her. 'But if I knew someone—'

'Will! Drop the subject, will you?' She gave him an exasperated look and made for the door. Didn't he ever take no for an answer? 'I'm happy. Charlie is happy. Now, if you'll excuse me I've got a surgery to take.'

'OK, OK, I'm sorry.' Will raised his hands in a gesture of surrender and smiled ruefully. 'You can't blame me for trying. Consider the subject dropped. Don't go yet—I need a quick word about a patient before we start surgery.'

Ally raised an eyebrow and paused with her hand on the doorhandle. 'One of yours or one of mine?'

'One of yours.' Will pulled a face. 'I was called out to little Kelly Watson last night. She had a dreadful asthma attack.'

'Again?' Ally sighed and closed the door again. 'This is the second time this month. Was she admitted?'

Will nodded and dragged a hand through his greying hair. 'Too right she was! Her mother was in a state of total panic, which didn't help. I spoke to the hospital today and they're going to increase the dose of inhaled corticosteroids before they discharge her.'

Ally frowned. 'She was on a reasonable dose—'

'If she was taking it.' Will stared at her, all traces of humour gone from his craggy features. 'I don't think she was.'

'But why?' Ally looked astounded. Why would a nine-year-old girl not take her medication when she knew what the complications were of not taking it? 'She's not exactly at the age of teenage rebellion.'

Will's mouth twisted. 'I don't know. I just think that the dose she was taking should have prevented that sort of attack. Have a chat to Lucy, will you?'

Lucy Griffiths, the practice nurse, ran an asthma clinic and knew all the patients better than anyone in the practice.

Ally nodded. 'Yes, of course. We obviously need to check her inhaler technique.'

'Thanks, Ally. Any news on young Pete Williams, by the way?'

Ally's eyes widened. Did everyone know? 'How did you know about Pete?'

'Never try and keep a secret from Uncle Will.' Will waggled his finger and then grinned. 'Actually, I met Jack in the Hare and Hounds last night. Sounded a pretty dramatic rescue.'

'Yes.' For a moment Ally's thoughts flew to Sean Nicholson and then she frowned. Why on earth had the man got to her so badly? 'Anyway, in answer to your question, I was planning to phone before I start surgery. I did try last night but he was still in Theatre.'

Will's face was suddenly serious. 'He's a good lad.'

Ally nodded, her voice soft. 'I know that. I'll have a long talk with him once he's up and about.'

'Do that. Oh, by the way...' He stopped her as she was about to leave, not quite meeting her eyes, 'Join me for lunch, will you? There's some practice business we need to discuss.'

Practice business? Ally gave a mental shrug and let the door swing closed behind her. Time enough for that later. What was happening to little Kelly Watson?

She found Lucy in the treatment room, preparing for the asthma clinic.

'I hear we've got problems with Kelly.'

Lucy nodded, her pretty face serious. 'Too right. I spoke to the registrar and he wants to increase her inhaled steroids, but I don't think that's the best approach, do you?'

Ally propped herself against the wall and frowned thoughtfully. 'When did we last check her inhaler technique?'

'Last time she had an attack.' Lucy flipped through her records. 'And we checked her peak flow. In fact, we went through her entire management plan. I was totally satisfied that both she and Mum understood what she had to do.'

'Well, something's badly wrong,' Ally murmured, ferreting around in her mind for a solution. 'Any ideas?'

Lucy understood the problems of the asthma patients better than anyone. 'Well, if I had to hazard a guess I'd say it was something to do with her mother.'

'Her mother?' Ally's eyes widened in surprise. 'Surely she wants her to be well?'

Lucy frowned and tapped her pen on the desk. 'You'd think so, wouldn't you? But she doesn't seem very keen on increasing Kelly's drugs.'

'Well, that's understandable, I suppose. No one likes taking drugs.'

'No.' Lucy stared at her thoughtfully and then shrugged. 'Well, anyway, I'll get them in and then let you know how I get on.'

'Brilliant.' Ally straightened and smiled. 'Thanks, Lucy. See you later.'

Her surgery was busy, a constant stream of coughs, colds and ear infections, and halfway through she snatched a moment to phone the hospital about Pete. Hearing that his condition was now stable, she breathed a sigh of relief. She'd have a thing or two to say to him when he was discharged! In the meantime, she made a mental note to visit him and take him something to cheer him up.

Her next patient was a young woman, thirty years of age, whom Ally remembered from her recent pregnancy.

'Hello, Jenny, how are the twins?'

Jenny Monroe smiled and rolled her eyes. 'Hard work and getting harder. They can't crawl yet but they've discovered that they can roll everywhere so I can't leave them alone for a minute.'

'I remember it well.' Ally sat back in her chair and laughed, her mind scooting back to when Charlie had been that age. 'Nightmare!' Only it hadn't been a nightmare. Not really. In many ways it had been wonderful, except for all the other traumas...

'My mother's got them for me for a few hours...' Jenny fidgeted slightly. 'I've got this thing on my leg and I've read so much lately about skin cancer it's been worrying me.'

'Let me have a look.'

Ally waited while Jenny pulled down her leggings, and then bent to examine the mole on her patient's leg. Alarm bells rang instantly in her mind. It had a jagged, uneven edge and was a mixture of black and brown, both signs highly suggestive of malignant melanoma.

'Are you a sunbather, Jenny?' She rummaged in her drawer for a ruler and measured the mole carefully.

Jenny looked sheepish. 'Well, not regularly, Dr McGuire, but I love the sun and I love to be tanned. It makes you feel better, doesn't it?'

It depended on your skin type, Ally thought wryly. When you were very fair, as she was, it was better to stay out of the sun altogether and settle for looking pale and interesting.

Ally frowned. 'Remind me where you work.'

'I'm a bank clerk.'

'And you holiday abroad?'

'Oh, yes!' Jenny smiled. 'Mike and I live for our two weeks of sunshine!'

An indoor job all year round and two weeks a year sunbathing—the very worst combination.

Jenny watched her curiously. 'Why are you measuring it?'

Ally hesitated and made a note on her pad. 'You were quite right to come and see me, Jenny, because suspicious moles do need to be checked out.'

'And this is suspicious?'

'It certainly needs to come off.'

Jenny swallowed. 'Do you think it's cancer?'

Ally hesitated. 'It's impossible to say, without removing it and examining the cells under a microscope.'

'But you think it might be, don't you?' Jenny probed, her eyes wide and anxious.

'It's possible,' Ally admitted, 'but we need to arrange for a specialist to remove the mole and have a proper look at it.'

'And if it is?' Jenny swallowed. 'What then?'

Ally reached over and gave her hand a squeeze. 'Jenny, it may be nothing. Why don't we wait for the results before we discuss the options?'

Jenny took a deep breath. 'OK. How long will I have to wait for an appointment? I won't sleep a wink until I know…'

'They're very quick,' Ally assured her, reaching for her hospital phone directory. 'I'll phone Mr Gordon, the plastic surgeon, today and he should see you this week.'

'Plastic surgeon? I thought it would be a dermatologist.'

'When it comes to removing moles it can be either. Mr Gordon is very good.'

Jenny gave her a shaky smile. 'Well, at least I won't have to wait long. Will I have to stay in hospital?'

Ally shook her head. 'No. They'll remove it under local anaesthetic as a day case and then ask you to go back for the results.'

Jenny nodded and stood up. 'Oh, well! Nothing to do but wait, then. Thanks, Dr McGuire.'

Ally watched her go and felt suddenly depressed. She was sure the mole would turn out to be malignant, and Jenny was a young woman with two small children…

Forcing those thoughts away, she phoned Mr Gordon's secretary and arranged for an urgent referral. Then she glanced at her watch, gasping as she saw the time. She was late for Will's meeting.

She flicked off her computer and hurried to the staffroom, stroking her wayward blonde curls back out of her eyes. Her hair hated being tied up for work and rebelled by gradually escaping from the tidy plait she started the day with. Maybe she should have replaited it before the meeting—but, then, it was only Will and the other partners and she was already late.

'Sorry, Will! I had two extras and—' She broke off and froze, her eyes fixed on the man lounging in one of the easy chairs. It was Sean Nicholson, freshly shaved and wearing stylish trousers and a jacket, a look of amused satisfaction pulling at the corners of his mouth as he watched her stunned reaction.

Will was looking as pleased as Punch with himself, although he didn't quite meet her eyes. 'There you are, Ally! I wanted to introduce you to our new locum.'

For a moment her heart flipped and words failed her.

With a slight smile Sean intervened, his voice that same deep, lazy drawl she remembered so well. 'We've met. Hello again, Ally.'

Had he known? Was that why he hadn't pressed her for her address? Because he'd somehow known he'd be working here with her? Had Jack said something? Suddenly she felt a shaft of panic. She didn't want to work with this man! He made her feel—feel—

'I didn't know you'd met—that's excellent.' Will was still smiling, gesturing for Ally to sit down. Her legs wouldn't move. 'Where did you meet?'

Ally didn't trust the innocent look on Will's face. And then she remembered that he'd met Jack for a drink, so he must have known about Sean...

'We met on the fells.' Sean was watching her closely, his dark eyes slightly narrowed. 'She was giving me advice on my abseiling.'

Will chuckled and placed a tray of coffee on the low table. 'I hadn't considered how much the pair of you have in common. That's excellent. It will make for a good working relationship.'

Good working relationship? Ally couldn't see herself having a good relationship with this man if she lived to be a hundred. He was everything she avoided in a man. Arrogant, handsome, chauvinistic—and totally compelling. She suppressed a groan. Work with him? Never! He made her too aware of herself and the feelings she'd squashed down for so long.

Sean was still watching her closely, his eyes intent. 'Have a sandwich, Ally.'

A sandwich? It would choke her!

'I thought you didn't approve of female doctors.' Ally found her voice at last and took refuge in sarcasm as she sat down in the nearest chair with a thump. Her legs were threatening to go on strike. It was sit down or fall down. 'Especially blonde ones.'

His appraisal was disconcertingly male. 'On the contrary, I totally approve of female doctors, especially if they're blonde.'

Ally ground her teeth and then caught the gleam of laughter in his eyes. Damn the man! He was winding her up again. Well, this time he wasn't going to succeed. Determined to look relaxed, she reached for a sandwich and concentrated her attention on Will instead.

'Sean's agreed to help us out until we can find a replacement for Tim,' Will said, looking more and more pleased with himself. 'He's just what we need in the team.'

'Dr McGuire may disagree.' Sean smiled slightly. 'She thinks I'm a chauvinist pig.'

'Well, I dare say you are a bit,' Will said calmly. 'All those years in the army, I suppose. But deep down women like a man to be a man.'

Ally ignored that bit. 'In the army? You did your medicine in the army?'

'No.' Sean shook his head. 'I trained after I left the army.'

She could see him in the army. Short, cropped hair and a slightly wonky nose which had obviously been on the receiving end of someone's fist—although, from what she'd seen of Sean, the other guy would have come off worse.

'So what's your special interest?'

'Trauma.'

Stupid question, Ally thought wryly, remembering his skill with Pete. That explained why he'd been so skilled and confident. And now she knew why Will wanted him.

'He's going to run our minor accident clinic?'

Will beamed. 'Absolutely.'

Ally's heart sank and then she gave a philosophical shrug. They did need someone badly and it wasn't as if she'd have to work that closely with him.

'Well, your trauma experience will be useful,' she said briskly, proud of how matter-of-fact and calm she sounded. 'We've been getting very busy since we agreed to see minor accidents here, instead of sending them all the way to the infirmary.'

Will nodded enthusiastically. 'We'll offer daytime cover for all minor emergencies, including weekends. People won't have to travel so far—it makes for a much more comprehensive service. And you're the perfect person.'

Sean's eyes narrowed. 'This is only temporary, Will…'

Will looked out of the window across the fells. 'Of course it is.'

Sean's mouth tightened for a moment and then he gave a short laugh. 'You're a manipulative old goat.'

Will smiled. 'Absolutely. I'll do anything to get what I want for my practice. And I want you, lad.'

'I would have thought general practice would be a bit tame after trauma,' Ally suggested, and Sean shrugged.

'So did I until that rescue the other day. Now I think it might have distinct possibilities.' He shot a warning glance at Will. 'As a temporary measure.'

So he obviously wasn't planning to stay for long. Thank goodness for that!

Ally sipped her coffee. 'I phoned the hospital about Pete and he's doing quite well.'

Sean helped himself to another sandwich. 'More than he deserves, then, taking those sorts of risks.'

Ally thought of Pete and the problems he'd had to face in his young life, and her blood boiled. 'Don't judge until you know what you're talking about,' she said tartly. 'People may have a good reason for taking risks.'

Like proving to themselves they could do it.

Sean shook his head, his tone cool and unemotional. 'Those boys could have killed themselves out there.'

And, in fact, if it hadn't been for Sean's skill Pete would undoubtedly have died, but Ally still couldn't bear him to make judgements about a person he didn't know.

'He was unlucky.'

'He was a fool.' Sean lobbed a crisp packet into the bin, his eyes hard. 'He shouldn't have been out in those conditions at all. And neither should you.'

'I wasn't taking risks, Dr Nicholson.'

'No?' His mouth tightened. 'You've all the bulk of an elf and you're roaming those hills in the middle of November on your own.'

'It's October,' she said sweetly, wondering why Will looked so pleased with himself. They were arguing, for heaven's sake! Shouldn't he be looking worried? 'And I don't see how obesity would help me survive in the fells. It's equipment and knowledge that count, not size. I know those hills and I don't take risks. I was the one who told you the safest place to abseil, remember? Jack knew I was out walking and he had my route. I had the dog with me and I had basic survival gear.'

His jaw tightened. 'If you were my woman I'd put a stop to it.'

Her heart tumbled in her chest and her breathing jerked.

'Well, I'm not your woman, Dr Nicholson.'

She clamped her hands in her lap and hoped he wouldn't see them shaking. What on earth was the matter with her? She didn't want to be his woman. She didn't want to be anybody's woman. All the men she'd met in her life had just been bad news. Selfish and egotistical and, from what she'd seen, Sean was no different. Get a grip! she told herself firmly. Goodlooking or not, he was still a man and that put him totally off limits. She'd had enough of men to last her a lifetime.

There was something in his eyes that she couldn't interpret and it made her nervous. He turned to Will. 'Did you know she wanders round the fells on her own?'

'Ally?' Will gave a philosophical shrug. 'Well, yes. She's lived here all her life and she knows these fells better than anyone.'

Sean frowned. 'And you think that qualifies her to gallivant off on her own with no back-up or equipment?'

Will shrugged and spooned sugar into his coffee. 'She's sensible and she's got Hero.'

Sean blinked. 'Hero?'

'Her German shepherd dog. She takes him everywhere.'

'Hero?' Suddenly Sean laughed out loud, his hard features softened by the smile. 'You called the dog Hero?'

Ally bristled. 'That's what he is to me.'

Sean watched her for a moment and then gave a small shrug. 'Well, dog or not, she shouldn't be walking alone, Will.'

Will helped himself to another sandwich. 'Try stopping her. Ally knows these mountains as well as anyone around here. She was in the mountain rescue team for years. I couldn't stop her walking any more than I could stop you, Sean.'

'Would you mind not talking about me as if I wasn't present?' Ally said indignantly, chewing a sandwich with limited enthusiasm. It tasted like sawdust. 'How do you know each other? And while you're at it, perhaps you'd better fill me in on how you know half the mountain rescue team as well.'

'I grew up here,' Sean said shortly, and she saw something slam shut in his eyes.

'And?'

He placed his coffee-cup carefully down on the table, his eyes cool and discouraging, all traces of humour gone. 'And what, Dr McGuire?'

'Well, there must be more to it than that.' She gave him a curious look, sensing the barriers he'd just erected. 'Did you go to school with Jack? Did Will deliver you as a baby?'

The smile faded from Will's face and he glanced warily at Sean.

'I didn't know you were so interested in me.' His handsome

face was taut, and she swallowed. Obviously Sean Nicholson did not want to talk about his past.

'Just making polite conversation,' she said quickly, wondering what had caused those shadows around his eyes. Whatever it was, Sean didn't want to talk about it. There was no doubt about that.

'Sean was working in Accident and Emergency last,' Will said quickly, smoothing over the tense atmosphere in the cosy staffroom. 'He's pioneered certain aspects of immediate care—stimulated by your army experiences, I suppose?'

Sean nodded and his shoulders relaxed slightly. 'That's right. When you're stuck in the field with an injured man you have to do the best you can with limited equipment.'

So that was why he'd handled the mountain rescue with such ease. And why Will had laughed when Sean had mentioned her abseiling tuition. 'I suppose you abseiled a lot in the army?'

His lips twitched. 'Just a bit.'

Will stretched his legs in front of him. 'Have you fixed somewhere to stay?'

'Not yet.' Sean pulled a face and helped himself to a sandwich. 'I plan to have a scout around this weekend. Unless you know of anywhere?'

Will concentrated on peeling an apple, not looking at Ally. 'Ally is looking for a lodger.'

Ally gasped. 'Will! I'm not! I—'

Will looked up, his expression unreadable. 'You told me you needed to get a lodger now that Fiona has gone back to London.'

'Well, I do, but not—I mean, that's different.' Ally licked her lips. She'd kill him! 'Fiona was a midwife—'

Sean contemplated her with silent laughter. 'I can deliver a baby if that's one of the requirements.'

'That's not what I meant and you know it.' Ally gritted her teeth. There was no way she was going to have this man lodging with her, even if she did need the money. He'd find out she'd misled him about her personal life for a start. The only person she was involved with was her daughter. And what would he do when he found that out? He needed to be kept at arm's length.

'What she means is she doesn't want me,' Sean murmured, his dark eyes challenging.

She shifted under his laughing gaze, hating the way he made her feel. As if she was a coward—which, of course, she was when it came to men.

'Of course she wants you. It makes sense, Ally,' Will said firmly. 'That barn drains every penny you earn.'

'Barn?' Sean was looking at her curiously. 'You live in a barn?'

'It's in the middle of nowhere and you'd hate it,' Ally said flatly, giving Will a threatening look which he met with a smile. Ally almost snarled. He was doing it again! Matchmaking! Trying to pair her up with anything male under the age of ninety. Why couldn't he just leave her alone?

'It's the perfect solution,' Will said happily. 'You need a lodger and Sean needs a place to stay.'

Ally opened her mouth to refuse for the final time and then caught the wistful look on Will's face and closed it again. Oh, blow the man! How could he do this to her? He had been so good to her for so long. In fact, without him she didn't know how she would have survived. She owed him so much and he made her feel churlish every time she avoided his attempts to liven up her life.

Maybe if she let Sean stay in her barn it would keep Will quiet. Stop his matchmaking. Prove to him once and for all that no matter how many men he paraded in front of her she wasn't interested. It just wasn't fair on Charlie. She needed constancy in her life, not a continual throughput of men who walked out when the going got tough. No, a lodger was all Sean would ever be, and even then it wasn't as if they would really be sharing accommodation. The stable wing attached to her barn was quite self-contained. All she had to do was pass him on the driveway occasionally.

'Do you mind sleeping in a stable?' Her voice sounded unwelcoming but Sean just smiled.

'Is the horse still in it?'

She gave him a withering look and the smile deepened.

Will stood up and deposited his mug and plate in the sink. 'Ally's stable is gorgeous—she's spent a lot of money converting it.'

'Has she now?' Sean's eyes meshed with hers and she forced herself to hold his gaze. 'And doesn't your husband mind having lodgers?'

'Oh, Ally's not married,' Will said blithely. 'Didn't I mention it?'

Thanks, Will! Ally thought, feeling her colour rise. Thanks a lot. Now that he'd well and truly set the scene she didn't know whether to laugh or kill him.

'But she lives with someone,' Sean murmured, giving her an odd look that she couldn't interpret.

'Lives with—? Well, yes, Charlie, but not...' Will glanced at Ally with a frown, which deepened as he met her pleading look. His mouth tightened. 'Oh, I see. Well, I've got calls to make so I'll leave the two of you to sort out the details.'

With that he left the room, leaving Ally gaping after him, boiling with frustration, knowing she'd been totally outmanoeuvred.

Sean stood up and made himself another cup of coffee. 'Subtle, isn't he? More coffee?'

'No, thanks.' Ally felt swamped with embarrassment by Will's obvious games. 'I don't know what's come over him.'

Sean gave a wry smile. 'Well, if that's really the case then I go back to my first impression of dizzy blonde. He's matchmaking, sweetheart, as you well know, and what *I* want to know is why he's matchmaking when you're already attached.'

Ally blushed furiously. 'I don't know.'

One dark eyebrow lifted. 'No?'

'No.' She started to clear away the remains of the sandwiches to hide her awkwardness. 'And, anyway, it's totally irrelevant because I wouldn't have a relationship with you if you were the last man on earth.'

Sean dropped into one of the chairs and stretched long legs out in front of him, his eyes amused. 'Is that so?'

She warmed to her subject. 'Yes, it is. You, Dr Nicholson, are the original male chauvinist pig who thinks that a woman's place is in the home, keeping it warm for her man. I don't suppose you've ever even heard of "New Man", have you?'

Sean smiled politely. '"New Man"?'

'Yes, you know—the sort of partner who respects women as equals, who doesn't mind doing the ironing or the washing-up and who certainly wouldn't stop me fell-walking if that's what I chose to do.'

Sean looked interested. 'You don't think I qualify as "New Man"?'

'You?' Ally gave a snort of derision. 'You're a clone of the original Stone-Age version. The only difference is that you wear clothes instead of a loincloth.'

His eyes gleamed with unholy laughter. 'Any time you want to see me in a loincloth, Dr McGuire, you only have to ask.'

Vivid images of Sean Nicholson with no clothes on flashed before her eyes and she coloured furiously. His smile deepened.

'You're the limit!' Her tongue moistened dry lips and her breath caught as his eyes dropped to her mouth.

'So why aren't you married, Dr McGuire?'

Ally lifted her chin. 'That's none of your business.'

His eyes met hers. 'Charlie obviously isn't Mr Right, then.'

'Let's get one thing straight, shall we?' Ally glared at him. 'You can move into my barn if you so wish because it would please Will and, frankly, I haven't the energy to argue, but don't read any more into it. You're my lodger. Nothing more.'

Sean raised an eyebrow. 'Have I asked for more?'

Ally blushed. 'Well, no, but—'

'I never touch another man's woman, and you've told me you're already involved with someone.' There was something benign about his expression that she didn't trust an inch. 'Aren't you?'

'Well, yes, but—'

'So that's that, then.' He drained his mug and stood up, his powerful figure dominating the small room. 'Of course, if you weren't involved with someone then the situation would be entirely different.'

His eyes held hers for a long moment and she swallowed uncomfortably. Had he guessed? What was going to happen when he found out that the person she was involved with was her daughter? She gave herself a shake. Nothing was going to happen. Nothing. Because she would make sure it didn't. She owed it to Charlie.

CHAPTER THREE

SURGERY was relatively quiet, courtesy of the extra pair of hands—a fact not missed by the patients.

'I see there's a new doctor!' One of Ally's regulars settled herself comfortably in the chair and looked expectant.

Ally suppressed a sigh of frustration. Some of her patients were wonderful but some of them were just downright nosy!

'That's right, Mrs Turner, we're glad to have the help.'

Mrs Turner fiddled in her handbag and pulled out a handkerchief. 'Will this one be staying longer than the last one, then?'

Ally forced a smile. She sincerely hoped not. With any luck he'd be moving on in a few weeks and she'd be able to breathe properly again.

'Dr Nicholson is a locum doctor. He's only temporary. Now then, what can I help you with today?'

The old lady looked momentarily baffled. 'Well, nothing, dear, I—'

'You came to see me, Mrs Turner,' Ally reminded her gently, and was rewarded with a smile.

'Of course! I remember now. My ears.' She shook her head gingerly. 'They're popping all the time.'

Ally picked up her auroscope and examined both her patient's ears carefully. 'There's nothing wrong, Mrs Turner, just a build-up of wax. Make an appointment with Sister to have them syringed. You need to put a few drops of olive oil into your ears for a few days before you see her.'

'Wax! Is that all?' The old lady looked at her suspiciously. 'Did you get a proper look?'

Ally smothered her smile. 'Wax can be very painful. If

there's no improvement after you've had them syringed, come back and see me.'

She watched Mrs Turner go with a wry smile, her mind only half on the job. The other half was on Sean Nicholson and how she was going to handle him. One thing was sure, he wasn't an easy man to brush off. Once he wanted something he got it. And was that her? With a groan she rubbed her aching forehead with her slim fingers and then summoned up a smile as her next patient tapped on the door.

Mary Thompson was a nervous lady in her late forties whom Ally usually saw only rarely. Lately she'd been visiting the surgery every few weeks, each time with something minor. Ally had a growing suspicion that something else was wrong.

'Hello, Mrs Thompson.' Ally smiled at her gently. 'What can I do for you today?'

The woman settled herself on the edge of the chair, her thin fingers twisting her gloves.

'I'm so sorry to bother you but I've had a bit of a cough, Doctor.'

Ally nodded and reached for her stethoscope. 'For how long?'

Mrs Thompson looked vague. 'Oh, a couple of weeks, I suppose—hard to say, really. But it's keeping me awake at night.'

A couple of weeks. A quick glance at the computer confirmed that she'd seen her only last week with a painful toe. If her chest had been bothering her then, why hadn't she mentioned it? Something nagged at Ally's brain.

'Slip your top off, Mrs Thompson, and let me have a listen to your chest,' she murmured, wondering how best to get to the bottom of this. She didn't know Mary Thompson that well and she didn't seem the sort to open up easily.

She listened to the woman's chest and found it clear, just as she'd suspected.

'Do you smoke, Mrs Thompson?'

Mary Thompson shook her head. 'No, Doctor, but my husband does.'

Her husband. Ally had a vague mental picture of an overweight man in his early fifties. Yes, that was him. She'd seen him once for a routine medical for a new job.

'Your chest doesn't sound too bad,' Ally said carefully, folding up the stethoscope and placing it back on her desk. 'I'd like to check it again in a week. Is there anything else I can help you with while you're here, Mrs Thompson?'

Was there just the briefest hesitation? 'No, Doctor. No, just my chest.'

Ally tried again, her voice infinitely gentle. 'Are you sure there's nothing else worrying you, Mary?'

The woman gripped her handbag until her knuckles were white. 'Nothing at all.'

So why didn't Ally believe her? 'I really would like to see you again next week.'

Mary Thompson nodded slowly and stood up, looking utterly defeated. 'If you think it's necessary.'

'I do,' Ally said firmly. 'I need to check that chest.'

She watched her patient leave with a feeling of helplessness. Something else was wrong, she knew, but if the patient wouldn't confide in her then there wasn't much she could do but wait. Unless she could find an excuse to call on her…

There was a tap on the door and Sean put his head round. 'I've finished surgery and I'm off on my rounds. If you're sure about renting me the stable, I'll pop in later.'

Ally gave him a brief nod, her mind still on Mary Thompson. As for the stable, she was far from sure about renting it to Sean, but it would keep Will off her back and she needed the money badly. Since Charlie's birth it had been a permanent struggle to make ends meet even on a very reasonable doctor's salary.

'I live just beyond Ambleside, past the turning for the Kirkstone pass.' She reached for a piece of paper and scribbled him a map. 'I'll be in after five.'

And her mother dropped Charlie home at 5.15. Confession time.

'Great.' Sean crossed the room and took the map from her. 'Everything OK? You look worried.'

'Oh—' She gave him a distracted look. 'Just a patient, that's all.'

To her consternation he dropped into the empty chair and stretched his long legs out in front of him.

'Want to talk about it?'

Talk about it? With him? Somehow she hadn't got used to the idea that this man was a doctor despite the skill with which he'd handled the casualty on the mountain.

'Not really.' She shook her head and then hesitated. Maybe another perspective would be worth having. 'Well, I mean, there's nothing to talk about, on the surface. It's just that I've got this feeling that she's desperate to tell me something and doesn't know how. I just know there's something going on.'

Sean raised an eyebrow. 'The "While I'm here, Doctor, can I just mention something else?" type of patient?'

'Exactly.' Surprised that he'd understood, Ally gave him a wary smile and bit her lip. 'Except Mary Thompson never does mention anything else. Just keeps consulting me about all sorts of ridiculous minor things...'

Sean frowned. 'Could she be depressed?'

Ally thought for a moment and shook her head. 'I don't think so.'

'Family problems?'

The mental picture of Mary Thompson's husband returned and Ally nodded slowly. 'Maybe. I just wonder if— Oh, I don't know! I'm probably imagining it and there's nothing else wrong at all.'

Sean gave a short laugh. 'In my experience the one thing you can rely on in life is your instincts. If they tell you there's something wrong then there probably is. I should follow it up.'

'But how?' Ally shrugged her shoulders helplessly. 'If she won't open up, I can hardly force her, can I?'

'Well, she obviously wants to or she wouldn't be consulting you all the time.' Sean stood up and tucked her map into his pocket. 'Why not invite her to a well woman clinic? Maybe that would be a more relaxed situation than a busy surgery.'

Ally thought for a moment. It wasn't a bad idea. If Mary Thompson didn't turn up to have her chest checked again, maybe she'd do just that. She smiled gratefully at Sean, surprised that something useful had come out of a conversation between them. Maybe she would be able to work with him after all. Maybe her brain was stronger than her hormones...

'Good idea—I might do that if she doesn't come back to see me next week.'

Sean studied her for a moment, his gaze leaving her heart thudding. OK, so maybe her hormones were winning at the moment. 'I'll see you later, then.'

She watched him go, nervously wondering whether she'd done the right thing, agreeing to let the stable to him. She'd shied away from men and relationships for so long she'd forgotten what it felt like to be living in close proximity to one. How would they get on together? Would she ever be able to relax and just get on with her life?

With a groan she flopped back in her chair and closed her eyes, trying to rationalise her fears. The stable was totally self-contained, she reminded herself firmly. She need hardly see him. She wouldn't even know he was there...

Her next patient tapped on the door and Ally pulled herself together quickly, pushing aside visions of those lazy dark eyes and firm mouth. She really had to concentrate.

Involving herself in her patients, she was surprised when she finally glanced at her watch and realised the time. Ouch! If she wasn't careful she'd be late for Charlie. She buzzed through to Helen, the practice manager.

'Any more for me, Helen?'

'No. Scoot off home to that girl of yours,' she replied. Ally smiled and turned off her computer. Helen was the backbone of the practice. She knew every patient and all their problems.

Not because she was nosy but because she was the sort of warm, caring person in whom everyone confided. Including Ally!

On the short drive home she drank in the stark outline of the fells, looming menacingly out of the dark, wondering whether Sean would have found his way.

He had.

The lights from her barn illuminated the powerful motorbike and the tall figure standing next to it, and she gave a short laugh. Of course, it had to be a motorbike. She should have guessed. Switching off the engine, she sat for a moment, dredging up the courage to leave her car. Horribly conscious of the way his leathers stretched lovingly across his wide shoulders and clung to the hard muscle of his thighs, she took a deep breath and stepped onto the gravel. Why did he have to be so devastatingly male? Why couldn't he have been a puny wimp?

'Hello, there.' Sean turned from his assessment of the barn and flashed her a smile that made her stop in her tracks. Black made him look like a bandit—dark, handsome and very, very dangerous. Hadn't he been clean-shaven in surgery earlier? So why was his hard jaw already blue with stubble? Obviously too many male hormones...

'I'm sorry if I'm late,' Ally babbled, averting her eyes and locking her car. Picking up her bag, she tucked it under her arm and scrunched over the gravel past her barn to the adjoining stable. 'I was held up in surgery.'

'No problem.' He tucked his helmet under one arm and waited while she fumbled for the keys, which promptly fell from her shaking fingers and landed with a dull thud on the gravel. Brilliant! So much for being cool and in control. Cursing under her breath, she stooped to retrieve them, catching the gleam of amused satisfaction in his eyes. Blow the man! He knew exactly what effect he was having on her and he was enjoying every minute of it.

'I expect you'll find it too isolated here,' she said crisply, ramming the key into the lock with more force than was necessary and pushing open the door quickly. She just couldn't begin to think of the effect he would have on her if he moved in. She'd need spare sets of keys to start with, to make up for all the ones she was going to drop...

'Still trying to put me off?' Sean's smile widened as he stepped in after her. 'I hate to disappoint you, but there's nothing I like more than isolation. I can't think of a better position. Just the sheep as neighbours.'

If it was just the sheep it wouldn't be a problem...

'Well, they can be pretty noisy.' Ally flicked on the lights and dropped her bag on the polished wooden floor, nerves making her brisk and formal. 'It's not very big—'

'You're a born salesman, Ally.' There was a wry gleam in his eyes as he walked slowly round the living area, tipping his head back to stare up into the eaves and then glancing at the gallery. 'What's up there?'

'The bedroom.' Catching his eye, Ally gritted her teeth. It wasn't going to work. It really, really wasn't going to work. She doubted whether she could live comfortably in the same country as this man, let alone the same property.

'I'll take it.'

Her mouth opened to tell him that she'd changed her mind, that he couldn't rent it, but her voice went on strike. She took a deep breath and tried again.

'You haven't seen the kitchen yet.'

'Don't tell me—no running water and rats in the cupboards?' Sean chuckled and strolled over to the huge glass window which stretched up into the eaves. His legs planted slightly apart, he stared into the darkness. 'This must be a view and a half. Which fells can you see in daylight?'

'The Langdales,' Ally muttered, averting her eyes from those powerful shoulders. He was standing directly in front of her and she was ridiculously aware of how close he was. Almost close enough to touch... She closed her eyes and cursed herself. She didn't want to touch him. Not even with the aid of a long bargepole. He was trouble. 'You get the same view from the bedroom.'

The minute she'd said it she could have bitten her tongue off.

Sean turned slowly and gave her a lazy smile which seriously compromised her heart rate. 'I'm not generally that bothered about the view from the bedroom.'

Ally's face coloured but she ignored the implication and walked briskly towards the kitchen. 'The bathroom's through there and this is the kitchen. It's not big but it should have everything you need.'

Sean stepped in behind her and immediately she wished she'd just left him to find it himself. This kitchen wasn't big enough for two people. At least not when one of them was Sean Nicholson.

'This place is fantastic. Did you convert it yourself?'

She shook her head. 'A local builder did it for me. Then I lived in here while he converted the barn next door.'

'He did a good job.' He tilted his head to look at the rafters. 'It's the perfect rental property, isn't it? Totally private.'

She hoped so. She sincerely hoped so. Living too close to this man would play havoc with her sanity. She must have been mad to let Will bully her into it. And why couldn't she bring herself to tell him she'd changed her mind?

'So you've had lodgers ever since you built it?'

'Yes.' She stared out of the kitchen window into the darkness. 'My parents owned it years ago, then they decided to sell most of the land around here and they gave my sister and me the barn.'

'But your sister doesn't live here now?'

Ally stood without moving. 'My sister died.'

There was a moment's silence. 'I'm sorry.'

'Don't be.' She blinked at the quiet sympathy in his voice and gave him a wan smile. 'It was a long time ago.'

'And the barn was derelict?' He strolled out of the kitchen

and ran a finger along the wall, following the line of the exposed brickwork.

She gave a short laugh and followed him, grateful that he hadn't dwelt on the subject of her sister. Maybe he had more sensitivity than she'd given him credit for. 'Oh, yes, completely derelict. Converting it was a massive job. Hence the lodgers.'

'When did your last lodger leave?'

'Fiona?' Ally closed the kitchen door and brushed a blonde strand out of her eyes. 'A month ago. She was offered a job in London and snapped it up. Like most people, she couldn't wait to get away from rural Cumbria.'

Sean glanced at her and raised an eyebrow. 'Most people maybe, but not you.'

She shrugged and walked over to the cosy living area. 'I was never a lover of bright lights and city streets even when I was young. I'm a mountain, outdoor type so this place suits me perfectly.'

'When you were young?' His mouth quirked and he leaned casually against the wall, watching her steadily. 'And you are now in your dotage, of course?'

Ally gave him a reluctant smile. She felt as old as the hills but maybe that was just inside. Obviously the trauma of recent events hadn't aged her externally.

'Well, let's just say I'm certainly past needing the excitement of a big city.'

'And what about other types of excitement, Ally? Are you past needing those, too?'

He wasn't leaning against the wall any more. Somehow he'd managed to move close to her without her even noticing. 'I'm happy with my life here, Dr Nicholson.'

Sean pulled a face. 'Can we drop the formality? You make me feel as though I'm in the middle of a ward round.'

She didn't want to drop the formality. Formality made her feel safer. First names made things more intimate and that was the last thing she wanted. 'I would have thought you liked formality, having been in the army.'

He shrugged those wide shoulders. 'I left, didn't I? Frankly, I was never really into hiding behind rank and titles. Not my style. So, are you going to let me rent this fabulous place or…' he paused slightly and his eyes gleamed '…do you need to check with Charlie?'

Charlie? Oh, goodness, she'd forgotten about Charlie! Why on earth had she misled him? She was going to have to confess before he found out for himself.

She swallowed. 'Dr Nicholson—I mean, Sean—there's something I ought to tell you—'

The sound of a car on the gravel outside interrupted them and she closed her eyes. Oh, great. Well, that was that. So much for her confession.

Sean glanced through the hall window. 'You've got visitors.'

Not visitors. Residents.

At that moment the door opened and Charlie rushed in, her hair flying and cheeks pink from the cold.

'Mum—what are you doing in here? There's a brilliant motorbike outside and—' She stopped dead when she saw Sean, her expression wary. 'Who's that?'

Ally swallowed, too flustered to comment on Charlie's lack of manners. 'This is Dr Nicholson, sweetheart. He's going to be working at the surgery for a while and Uncle Will thought he could stay in our stable. Where's Grandma?'

'She said to tell you she'd ring you later. She's gone because Princess is calving. I wanted to stay but she said no.' Charlie stared at Sean. 'Is that your motorbike?'

'It is.' Sean returned her gaze steadily, his face expressionless as his eyes flickered over the blonde hair and huge blue eyes.

'Can I have a ride on it?'

'No, you can't!!' Ally said quickly, careful not to catch Sean's eye. 'Come on, let's go next door. If you hurry up you can still catch *Blue Peter*.'

'Aren't you going to introduce us?' Sean's voice was velvety smooth and Ally took a deep breath and forced herself to look at him. It was a mistake. Her heart slammed against her chest as she met those dark eyes.

'This is my daughter, Charlotte.'

'Known as Charlie, no doubt.'

Charlie stared at him. 'How did you know that?'

Sean's eyes were still on Ally. 'Call it intuition.'

'What's intu—?'

'Just go next door, Charlie,' Ally interrupted quickly, stooping to pick up the abandoned schoolbag in an attempt to conceal her flushed face. 'We've finished in here anyway, so I'll just get Dr Nicholson the keys and then he can move in when he likes.'

'Great.' Charlie bounced out in front of them. 'Wait till Karen sees that motorbike.'

Ally locked the door with trembling hands, aware that Sean was still watching her. When she risked a glance in his direction her heart tumbled frantically. Dear God, why did the man make her so nervous? She'd met attractive men before and not even given them a second glance. Why was Sean Nicholson different? Why did he affect her so badly? Still, at least this time she hadn't dropped the keys. With a huge effort she pulled herself together. He was just a man. A handsome one maybe, but a man nonetheless, with all the selfish, self-centred attributes that went with the territory. She could handle him. She could.

She unlocked the door of the barn and Hero bounded up, tail wagging. Charlie immediately shot off to her bedroom, dragging the dog with her, leaving her alone with Sean.

Her heart thudding in her chest, Ally walked briskly over to the kitchen and tugged open one of the drawers.

'You'll need a set of keys.'

Sean lounged in the doorway, his eyes flickering briefly to the keys that she dropped onto the kitchen table. 'So you're happy for me to move in, then?'

'Happy?' Ally closed the drawer with a thump. 'No, I'm not

happy. I'm letting you move in because of Will so let's be clear about that right from the start.'

Sean straightened and his firm mouth moved slightly. 'Because of Will?'

'Yes!' Damn the man. How dared he stand there, looking so arrogantly handsome and amused? He obviously thought she couldn't wait for him to move in. 'I happen to owe Will a lot and I don't want to hurt his feelings.'

Sean scooped up the keys and jangled them in his palm. 'And what's me moving in got to do with Will's feelings?'

Ally glanced at him briefly and then coloured and bit her lip. 'Because he thinks he's matchmaking and I haven't the heart to disillusion him.'

'Ah, now I see.' Sean pocketed the keys and his eyes gleamed. 'You're saying that you're prepared to have a wild affair with me to spare Will's feelings.'

'Oh, very funny.' She gritted her teeth. 'You know very well that's not what I'm saying.'

'You're not?' He raised an eyebrow, his eyes dancing wickedly, and she resisted the temptation to thump him. Instead, she wrapped her arms round her slim body and glared at him.

'This isn't a joke, Sean!'

'Am I laughing?'

'Yes,' she growled fiercely, 'and you have no idea what it's like to be constantly on the receiving end of everyone's matchmaking attempts.'

'Well, that's where you're wrong.' He gave a short laugh and dropped onto one of the kitchen chairs, his legs stretched out in front of him. 'I know exactly what it's like.'

'You?' She shot him a look of pure disbelief. 'You must have women coming out of the woodwork.'

He shrugged and pulled a face. 'Maybe. But I certainly don't intend to marry any of them just to please my friends.'

She stared at him. 'And that's what they want you to do?'

He nodded ruefully. 'Especially Will. Which is why I don't visit them as often as I should.'

Ally removed a wisp of blonde hair from her eyes. 'Right, well, in that case it should be easy. Once Will sees we can resist each other perhaps he'll give up interfering.'

Sean rubbed his dark jaw and frowned thoughtfully. 'There's just one problem…'

'Which is?'

He gave a lazy grin and rose to his feet. 'I'm not sure I can resist you.'

For a moment she was hypnotised by the look in his laughing eyes and then she came to her senses. 'Oh, don't be so ridiculous!'

'What's ridiculous about it? I find you very attractive.'

Her heart was beating a strange rhythm. 'Well, the feeling isn't mutual.'

'You're a rotten liar.' His voice was soft, seductive and very, very male. 'I was hoping you were going to suggest some serious public canoodling just to keep Will happy.'

'In your dreams, Sean!'

'Well, that just shows how little you know about my dreams.' His wicked grin faded. 'Believe me, none of the dreams I've been having about you could ever be played out in public, Ally McGuire.'

She swallowed hard. 'Sean, please…'

'Please, what?'

'Just leave me alone.'

'No.'

'Oh, for goodness' sake!' She bit her lip and threw him a look that was half impatient, half desperate. 'There must be plenty of women out there who'd faint if you just smiled at them. Why not pick on one of them? Why me?'

'Why?' His eyes locked on hers. 'Because you're gutsy and beautiful and because you're fighting me every inch of the way.'

In other words, she was the first woman he'd ever met who'd refused him. She lifted her chin.

'Denting your ego, am I, Dr Nicholson?'

He threw back his head and laughed. 'Oh, no, Dr McGuire. My ego isn't that fragile.'

He was standing only inches away from her and she was finding it harder and harder to breathe normally.

'I'm not interested in what you're offering, Sean.'

To her relief he didn't come any closer. Instead, he rested one strong thigh on her kitchen table and looked at her thoughtfully. 'And what am I offering?'

She turned away, flustered, and started getting things ready for Charlie's tea. 'I don't know—a quick fling, a roll in the hay.'

'You want marriage?' His dry tone made her blood boil.

'Dammit, don't you listen?' She whirled round to face him, her heart thumping, her blonde hair wafting down over her smooth cheeks. 'I don't want anything! I don't want a fling, I don't want marriage, I just don't want any sort of relationship. Not with you, not with anyone.' She broke off, her breathing uneven, and he looked at her steadily.

'That bad, hmm?'

Ally looked at him blankly. 'What do you mean, "that bad"?'

'Your relationship with Charlie's father.'

Her shoulders stiffened. 'My relationship with Charlie's father is none of your business.'

'I disagree.' He studied her calmly. 'If it put you off men for life then I have a right to know what he did to you.'

Ally turned away and dragged a saucepan out of the cupboard. 'You have no rights. No rights at all. And what happened with Charlie's father is history.'

'History?' She heard the sudden coolness in his tone. 'You mean she doesn't see her father?'

'No.' Ally slammed the saucepan down on the hob and glared at him. 'No, she doesn't.'

He was frowning. 'You think it's right to keep a child away from her father?'

She ground her teeth and anger blazed out of her eyes. 'You're doing it again, Dr Nicholson. Jumping to conclusions.'

He shrugged. 'Wasn't he interested in being a father?'

'Rob? The only thing Rob was interested in was himself.' Ally didn't want to think about Charlie's father and how much pain he'd caused her entire family.

Sean was watching her closely. 'But you must have loved him at one time?'

Loved him? Rob the rat? He had to be joking! But, then, Sean didn't know the whole story, and she certainly wasn't about to tell him. She was keeping her distance.

'Everyone makes mistakes,' she said shortly, rummaging in the vegetable rack for an onion.

'And the child pays the price.' Sean's voice was suddenly hard and she gasped at the injustice of his remark, slamming the onion down on the work surface and whirling to face him.

'You always judge people before you know the facts, don't you?' She jerked her head angrily, her blonde hair flopping gently onto her shoulders as it finally escaped from the restraining plait.

He shrugged those broad shoulders, unconcerned by her outburst. 'So tell me the facts.'

'I have no intention of telling you the facts.' She glared at him. 'The facts are none of your business, Sean Nicholson, but don't you dare imply that Charlie has suffered from being with me because I can assure you that I give her everything a child needs.'

A muscle worked in his cheek. 'Except her father.'

'Yes, well, in Charlie's case she's better off without him!' Ally turned back to the onion and chopped it with fierce, deliberate strokes of the knife. The man made her so angry!

'Maybe a child is better off with a mediocre father than no father.'

'Well, that shows how little you know about the situation.' Controlling her temper with difficulty, Ally turned and dropped the knife into the sink, turning on the taps with more force than was necessary. 'My daughter may only have me, but at least I'm always here for her. I don't change my mind if I've had a tough day, and I don't give her up if something better comes along—'

'Is that what Charlie's father did?'

She turned to look at him, her eyes blazing. 'Charlie's father was a complete rat.'

His gaze was ironic. 'Well, you obviously didn't think he was that bad when you slept with him.'

The sound of her hand connecting with his lean cheek echoed around the kitchen, and she froze with the shock of her own actions. She'd hit him. Dear God, what had got into her? She'd never hit anyone or anything in her life before.

Breathing unsteadily, their eyes met, hers wide and shocked, his thoughtful and intent.

She blushed with mortification. 'I'm sorry...' she began stiffly, and he gave a short laugh, rubbing his cheek with a rueful expression in his eyes.

'Don't be. I deserved it. It was a totally insensitive comment.'

But it was the obvious comment—that she'd loved Rob enough to sleep with him and bear his child. Still shocked by her own actions, she covered her mouth with shaking fingers, her hand still tingling from the contact with Sean's cheek. For a moment she was severely tempted to blurt out the whole truth but then she stopped herself. Why on earth would she confide her life story to this man whom she hardly knew? She didn't want to confide in him. Didn't want to get close.

'It—it isn't how it seems. It's complicated. Rob was a total mistake,' she said briefly, her blue eyes wary as they watched him. It was the truth. Economical maybe, but the truth nonetheless.

He raised his hands in a comical gesture of surrender. 'Well, as you rightly said, it isn't any of my business.'

'No.' Ally stared at his cheek and bit her lip as she saw the livid red streak. 'I hurt you. What can I do? Do you want ice or something?'

He gave her a half-smile that was so sexy her knees almost gave way. 'You could kiss it better...'

Her breath clogged her throat. 'Don't be silly.' Her voice cracked slightly and she changed the subject quickly. 'So, what makes you feel so strongly about the subject of absent fathers?'

His jaw tightened and his expression was suddenly guarded. 'I just happen to believe that in an ideal world children should have two parents.'

She gave a short laugh and tipped the onion into a frying-pan, stirring it gently. 'Yes, well, this isn't an ideal world.'

'I'm well aware of that.'

'So you believe in happy ever after and Father Christmas, do you?'

He laughed. 'And the Easter Bunny? I'm afraid not. I believe in happy while it lasts.'

She frowned, still stirring the onion. 'But you just said children should have two parents.'

'Absolutely.' His voice was a lazy drawl. 'I just don't happen to believe you should have children unless you're one hundred per cent committed to each other. It isn't fair on the child.'

'But no one ever knows how a relationship will work out.'

'True. But once you have children you have a responsibility to make it work for their sakes. You just can't afford to be selfish.'

Ally stopped stirring. 'You're saying I'm selfish.'

'I'm not saying anything of the sort.' His voice was quiet. 'As you rightly pointed out, I know nothing about your circumstances and it's none of my business.'

'So you think it's OK to flit from one woman to another as long as there are no children involved?'

He frowned. 'I don't think "flit" would be the word I'd use but, yes, I think it's realistic to expect to change partners. It's better to acknowledge that rather than keep up this pretence of believing that you're going to be together for ever and making selfish decisions based on that fantasy.'

Ally dropped the spoon and glared at him. 'And it doesn't matter who gets hurt in the process? That's totally irresponsible!'

'On the contrary, it's extremely responsible.' His gaze clashed with hers and his mouth was a grim line, all traces of humour gone. 'Far more so than having children without any thought for their future. When my relationships end no one gets hurt.'

Was he kidding? Ally was willing to bet he'd left a trail of broken hearts around the country. Adult ones, maybe, but still. 'But don't you ever have dreams of a family of your own?'

'No, I don't.' He gave a short laugh, his expression grim. 'I gave up believing in fairy tales when I was still in nappies. I was determined never to be responsible for a child's unhappiness.'

She stared at him defensively. 'Charlie isn't unhappy.'

'I wasn't talking about Charlie.' He stared out of the window into the darkness, his expression unreadable. 'Charlie's obviously one of the lucky ones, but I know plenty of children who aren't so lucky.'

'But don't you ever want children of your own?'

'No.' Sean's eyes were shuttered. 'I don't.'

Ally stared at him and wondered what had happened in his life to bring him to that decision. Looking at his taut profile, she felt a surge of sadness which she quickly dismissed. Why feel sad that a man she hardly knew didn't want children? So what? Why should that affect her? Her eyes rested on his hard jaw and lifted to his eyes, and for some unfathomable reason the bleak look she saw there made her want to hug him. Hug him? She must be going mad. She shook herself mentally and pulled a can of chopped tomatoes out of the cupboard. Anything to keep her hands busy so that she didn't do something stupid.

'Anyway, talking of relationships...' The smile was back,

along with a wicked glint in his eye that she didn't trust an inch. 'What are we going to do about the chemistry between us?'

'Chemistry?' Her heart gave a jump and she moved quickly, putting the table between them as protection as he walked purposefully towards her. 'Don't kid yourself! I don't think exchanging arguments and insults can really be called chemistry.'

'Then why are you hiding behind a table?' Those dark eyes teased her as he moved closer. 'Who is it you don't trust? Yourself or me?'

Ally took a deep breath and gripped the back of a chair. 'Look, Sean, you've just said you avoid relationships, so—'

He grinned. 'Don't twist my words. I may avoid marriage and children, but I'm totally in favour of relationships.'

With her? He had to be joking! She wasn't that stupid...

'Well, I'm not.' How come her voice sounded so steady? 'It's not fair on Charlie.'

He raised an eyebrow in an expression of disbelief. 'You're expecting me to believe that you've lived like a nun since she was born?'

She almost laughed. He didn't know the half of it!

'Believe what you like, but leave me alone, Sean.' She looked away from him. 'It wouldn't work.'

Strong fingers grasped her chin and forced her to look at him. 'Give me one good reason.'

'I already have. Charlie.'

He stared at her for a long moment and then his hand dropped and he frowned. 'You're serious? You don't date men because of your daughter?'

Ally turned away and stirred the Bolognese sauce. 'Whatever you may think about the mistakes I made in Charlie's past, I intend to make sure there aren't any more in the future.'

'And I'd be a mistake?'

'Oh, yes. A huge mistake.' She wasn't the sort of person he obviously thought she was. The truth was she'd never had a fling with anyone before in her life. Never. She was one of those idiots who still believed in fairy tales and Father Christmas, and one special love that lasted for ever. Sean didn't. They were as different as chalk and cheese, and to pretend otherwise would lead to nothing but disaster. He might be attractive but he was also dangerous. Dangerous because he'd made it clear that he didn't want commitment, but for the first time in her life she was sorely tempted to put her principles to one side and take whatever was on offer.

But it wasn't going to happen, she told herself firmly. No matter how many times those dark eyes captured hers or that smile turned her insides to a pool of jelly. It wasn't going to happen. It wasn't fair on Charlie.

For all his easy charm Sean was too cool and detached for her. He obviously avoided any real intimacy. The sort of man who wouldn't think twice about having a brief affair and then moving on. He'd made that perfectly plain and chemistry or no chemistry she wasn't fool enough to think she'd be the one to change him.

She'd had enough of men who ducked responsibility. She was better off on her own. At least then no one could let you down.

'You've got the keys, so just go.' She kept her back to him, aware that he was standing only inches behind her. With a huge effort she made her voice crisp and businesslike. 'You can live in my stable, Sean, but that's all.'

His voice was soft and disturbingly close. 'For now.'

'For ever,' she said firmly, gripping the spoon tightly and praying that he'd leave.

There was a long silence and then she heard his soft laugh and the click of the door as he closed it quietly behind him.

CHAPTER FOUR

SATURDAY surgery was as busy as ever, which was just as well, Ally reflected wryly, because it stopped her thinking about Sean. Ever since he'd moved into the stable she just hadn't been able to concentrate on anything, even though she'd managed to avoid him very successfully. Apart from hearing the roar of his motorbike early in the morning, she was barely aware that he'd been living next to her for two days. And now he was next door again, this time running Will's minor accident surgery in the treatment room.

With a groan and a shake of her head Ally pressed the buzzer for her next patient who came in, clutching the hand of a fractious toddler.

'Hello, Felicity, how's the pregnancy?'

Felicity rolled her eyes and sagged into the chair, picking up a toy from Ally's box. 'Here we are, Tom, choo-choo train.'

The little boy took the train and plopped down on the floor contentedly. Felicity gave Ally a tired smile.

'The pregnancy, did you say? I don't know. I haven't got time to think about it. This little one and his older brother keep me too busy.'

Ally gave her a sympathetic smile. 'I'll bet. Not like the first time around, is it?'

'You can say that again.' Felicity gave a short laugh. 'The first time around I felt special. "Put your feet up, pet," Hugh used to say. He used to cook, clean, bring me tea in bed...'

'But not any more?'

Felicity laughed and passed Tom a bag of bricks which he cheerfully upended, before bursting into noisy sobs.

'Definitely not any more.' Felicity stooped to pick up the little boy, murmuring soothing noises as she bounced him on her knee. 'Anyway, believe it or not, I didn't come to moan! This little fellow is very out of sorts and he's got a nasty rash. I think it might be chickenpox because there have been a few cases in his nursery.'

'Let's have a look at him.' Ally picked up a puppet from her desk. 'Tom? Look what I've got…'

She jiggled the puppet until Tom started to chuckle and then handed it over to Felicity while she examined the little boy quickly but thoroughly.

'When did the rash start?' She listened to Tom's chest and checked his throat and ears.

'About three days ago, but he only had a couple of spots so I wasn't sure.'

Ally examined the rash carefully and then helped pull Tom's jumper back over his head.

'It's definitely chickenpox,' she confirmed, turning to her computer and tapping keys. 'I'll give you a prescription for Piriton syrup, which should help the itching.'

'When is he infectious, Dr McGuire—and should I keep him away from other children?'

Ally nodded. 'Most nurseries prefer you to keep them off although, in fact, they're infectious for twenty-four hours before the rash appears so in reality the chances are that he's already passed it on. But keep him off until the rash crusts over.'

'How long does that take?'

'About five days.' Ally waited while the computer printed out the prescription and then handed it to the mother. 'What we do need to talk about is you.'

'Me?' Felicity shifted Tom to the other knee and looked surprised. 'Why me?'

'How pregnant are you now?'

'Nearly thirty-seven weeks.'

'Right—and have you had chickenpox?'

Felicity screwed up her face and shrugged. 'I haven't got a clue, frankly. Why?'

'Because we need to take blood to check your immune status.'

Felicity frowned. 'But why? I know these infections are dangerous at the beginning, but the baby is formed by now, isn't it?'

'It is fully formed and you're right to say infectious diseases are dangerous in the beginning, but chickenpox is also a risk to the pregnant mother at the end of pregnancy.' Ally opened a drawer and pulled out a form. 'We need to check your immunity and then give you an injection if necessary.'

Felicity looked stunned. 'I'm glad I came now—I almost didn't because I was so sure it was just chickenpox.'

'I'm sure it won't be a problem,' Ally said firmly, scribbling Felicity's details on the form. 'Just take this to Sister next door and she'll take some blood from you. We'll ring you as soon as we have the results. But if you go into labour early, you give us a ring.'

'Will do.' Felicity stood up awkwardly and patted her lump. 'Why did I do it? Two was enough really, and I'm dreading the labour.'

Ally checked the notes. 'You had a forceps delivery last time.'

'And a ventouse the first time. I couldn't sit down for a month.' Felicity bit her lip. 'They say it gets easier but I'm not convinced.'

'It's very unusual to need forceps the second time around,' Ally told her. 'I'm sure this time you'll be fine. The presentation is good and you're very healthy.'

'Well, Hugh's having the snip after this one,' Felicity said with a mock scowl, and Ally smiled as she left the room.

Lucy bounced in five minutes later. 'I've just taken blood from Felicity Webster—could that chickenpox be bad news, do you think?'

Ally shook her head and smiled. 'She's probably immune—most people are.'

Lucy frowned and plopped herself in the empty chair. 'What if she isn't?'

'She has to be given ZIG.'

Lucy laughed. 'What on earth is ZIG? It sounds like something from outer space.'

'Zoster immune globulin,' Ally told her, slipping off her shoes and curling her slim legs under her bottom. 'Instant immunity.'

'Well, you learn something new every day. Anyway, enough of that.' Lucy gave her a curious smile. 'Who's this new locum we've got?' The door opened and Lucy turned her head, her jaw dropping as she stared at the man standing there.

'This is the new locum,' Ally said quickly, slipping her feet back into her shoes—but not before Sean had taken a long, leisurely look at her exposed thighs. Damn the man! 'Dr Nicholson, this is our practice nurse—'

'Lucy Griffiths,' Sean interrupted with a wry grin, and Lucy gasped and clapped her hand over her mouth.

'Sean?' With an unladylike shriek she scrambled off her seat and hurled herself into Sean's arms.

Sean hugged her back, his hard features softened by affection as he stooped to kiss her on the cheek.

'You've grown up.'

'Yes.' Lucy gave him a bright smile and pulled away from him, the warmth she felt for him evident in the glow of her eyes.

Did everyone know him? For a moment Ally felt a stab of emotion she didn't recognise. Jealousy? Surely not—why would she be jealous of Lucy? It wasn't as if she herself wanted Sean, and Lucy deserved to find someone.

'Oh, fancy it being Sean!' Lucy turned to Ally with a beaming smile which Ally managed to return. 'I never thought you'd come back here!'

Sean gave a short laugh. 'I was coerced.'

Lucy giggled deliciously. 'By Will?'

'By Will.'

Ally glanced between them. Obviously they knew each other well. She told herself off firmly for minding. Why on earth should she mind? Stupid!

'Where are you staying?' Lucy was still beaming and Sean stepped inside the room and closed the door behind him.

'With Ally.'

Ally dredged up a smile. 'He's renting my stable.'

Lucy's eyes widened. 'Gosh, you're honoured. Ally never usually rents to men.'

'So I gather.' Sean's eyes met Ally's. 'Let's just say that she was coerced, too.'

Lucy's jaw dropped. 'Will again?'

Ally managed a smile. Just. 'You guessed it.'

'He should run a dating agency!' Lucy giggled and glanced from one to the other. 'Isn't he sweet?'

'Irresistible,' Sean drawled sarcastically, glancing at his watch with a quick frown. 'I need to get on but I wanted to talk to you, Ally…'

She stiffened. She had nothing to say to him. Nothing. 'I'm in the middle of surgery.'

He raised an eyebrow. 'About a patient.'

She blushed and fiddled with her pen. 'Oh—right. What's the problem?'

'That woman you mentioned to me a few days ago…' He leaned broad shoulders against the doorway and frowned. 'Wasn't her name Thompson?'

'Mary Thompson.' Ally stared at him. 'What about her?'

'I may have found a clue to her problems.' Sean tossed a newspaper onto her desk and made for the door. 'Read the report on page four. It might shed some light.'

'Thanks.' Ally watched as he closed the door behind him and then reached for the paper, noticing that it was the local newspaper. Page four, he'd said hadn't he? Her eyes scanned the different stories. PRIMARY SCHOOL WINS AWARD FOR DESIGNING POSTER. OLD LADY MUGGED WHEN SHOPPING. She frowned as her eyes focused on a small piece at the bottom of the page—MAN CHARGED WITH DRUNKEN DRIVING.

'What is it?' Lucy peered over her shoulder and gave a low whistle. 'Ouch. Lost his licence and he's an insurance salesman. I suppose that means he's lost his job, too, does it?'

'If he needs the car for work then I suppose so,' Ally murmured, putting the paper down. She was sure that Sean was right. This probably was the key to the problem. Was Mary's husband an alcoholic or was the driving ban just a one-off? Either way she was going to have to handle it very tactfully.

She buzzed through to Helen and asked her to check whether Mary Thompson had booked another appointment.

'Four o'clock on Thursday' came the reply, and Ally made a note in her diary. It could wait until then.

'Good for Sean,' Lucy commented, making for the door. 'You know, you must be the envy of every woman in Britain, having that hunk living next door.'

Ally frowned impatiently. 'He's just my lodger.'

'Don't fall in love with him, Ally,' Lucy said softly. 'Sean's the most gorgeous man you could ever meet but he's not the settling-down type and you don't need more of that type of hassle.'

As if she needed warning! 'Are you speaking from experience?'

'No!' Lucy shook her head, her hand on the door. 'I was at school with him for a while, although he was years ahead of me.'

'What was he like?' Ally hated herself for asking the question but somehow she couldn't stop herself.

Lucy pulled a face. 'The original "bad boy". All the girls were crazy about him.'

Ally smiled wryly. Why didn't that piece of information come as a surprise? 'Including you?'

Lucy gave a wry smile. 'Well, I can't claim not to find him attractive, but there's something about him that ties me in knots and makes me nervous. He's incredibly tough and self-reliant, and I like my men a little more approachable.'

Ally frowned. 'I know what you mean. He's a total male chauvinist pig.'

Lucy gave a short laugh. 'Well, he's certainly all man if that's what you mean.'

All man. You could say that again. 'But you're really fond of him…'

'I owe him a lot.' Lucy fiddled with the doorhandle and took a deep breath. 'I was badly bullied for a while at school, and in the end it was Sean who sorted them out.'

Ally sat back in her chair, her eyes wide. 'What did he do?'

Lucy gave a short laugh, her eyes shadowed. 'Well, let's just say they never bullied anyone again after he'd finished with them.'

The intercom buzzed and Ally answered it, glancing at her watch as Helen asked her to see an extra.

'No problem—I haven't got that many calls so send them in.' She gave an apologetic smile to Lucy. 'Back to the grindstone.'

Lucy tugged open the door and stared at Ally thoughtfully. 'On second thoughts, ignore what I just said. You might be just what Sean needs.'

Just what Sean needs? What did he need? And what about what she needed? Ally stared after her and then blinked as the door opened and Jack entered.

'Jack?' She smiled in surprise and pulled herself together rapidly. 'I wasn't expecting you.'

He gave a rueful smile. 'I know, and I feel really guilty bothering you with this on a Saturday…'

Ally dismissed his apologies quickly. 'Saturday surgery is just like any other, Jack, you know that. Will was sensitive to the fact that so many people can't get to the doctor in the week, and it certainly cuts down the number of house calls we make at a weekend, so don't feel guilty. What's the problem?'

Jack pulled a face. 'Pains in my chest—awful, burning pains.'

Ally frowned and questioned him in detail about the pain, making notes as she did so.

'And does it go when you eat?'

'Funnily enough, yes.' Jack nodded thoughtfully. 'Is it an ulcer?'

'Maybe. I need to examine you properly.' Ally questioned him further on the exact nature of the pain and then examined him carefully.

'I can't feel anything abnormal, Jack,' she said finally as she washed her hands and waited for him to get dressed. 'And your symptoms do sound like a gastric ulcer.'

Jack dressed quickly and settled himself back in his chair. 'So now what?'

'Well, you need to try an antacid to start with, and you must take it four times a day. If that doesn't help then we'll give you something stronger. I've got a leaflet here on lifestyle advice.' She rummaged in her drawer and handed it to him with a grin. 'You won't like it.'

Jack gave a snort and scanned the leaflet briefly. 'You're going to tell me not to drink, aren't you?'

Ally laughed. 'Well, it is an irritant so at least cut down. We'll see how you get on. I might need to send you for a gastroscopy.'

'Looking into my stomach?'

She nodded. 'That's right. I'm sure it's straightforward, but as you're over forty-five and this has come on suddenly it's best to be on the safe side.'

'OK. I put myself in your hands.' He grinned and stood up. 'Thanks, Ally. By the way, are you and Charlie coming to the fundraising bonfire party next Saturday?'

'If I'm not on call.' Ally flicked through her diary and smiled. 'No, here it is. "Mountain Rescue Team party." By the way, try and restrict your conversation in front of Charlie, would you? I've spent the whole week answering questions on hypothermia and people dying on mountains.'

'Oops, sorry.' Jack looked guilty and walked towards the door. 'I was talking to your mum and I forgot she was there, actually. Oh, I gather Sean's living with you.'

Ally ground her teeth. News travelled fast in a small community. 'He's my lodger.'

'Right.' Jack's eyes gleamed slightly. 'Well, if you see him before I do, get him to come along, too, will you?'

She forced a smile. 'If I see him.'

She certainly wouldn't be going out of her way to find him. And she certainly wouldn't be going with him to a bonfire party.

Ally finished her calls fairly quickly and resisted the temptation to drop in on Mrs Thompson. There was a chance she'd make things worse by calling unannounced, and as the woman was coming to see her on Thursday she made the decision to be patient. Instead, she drove along the dual carriageway to the Infirmary to visit Pete Williams.

He was lying, immobilised, on the bed, his head buried in a book on climbing.

'Hello, trouble.' Ally dropped a football magazine on the bed next to him and settled herself in the chair.

'Dr McGuire!' His face brightened as he picked up the magazine. 'Hey, this is great! Thanks!'

'How are you feeling?'

'Sore.' Pete coloured. 'And very stupid. Mr Morgan read me the Riot Act.'

Ally gave him a sympathetic smile. 'You had a lucky escape.'

'I know.' His fingers fiddled with the sheet. 'Mr Morgan said that if you and Dr Nicholson hadn't been in the area I would have died.'

'Well, we were,' Ally said briskly, 'so don't let's think about things like that now. How's the blood sugar?'

He shrugged and pulled a face. 'Not too bad, considering.'

'What were you trying to prove, Pete?' Ally's voice was soft and Pete stared down at the bedcovers.

'Dunno, really.' He made an impatient sound. 'Yes, I do! I'm just fed up with it all, Dr McGuire. Being different, you know?'

Ally shook her head. 'No, I don't know. You're not different, Pete. You just have diabetes.'

'But that makes me different, doesn't it?' He glanced at her and then sagged back against the pillows. 'I can't join in cross-country properly because I have to test my blood sugar, I can't binge on food…'

Ally watched him thoughtfully. 'Well, the bingeing probably isn't a good idea, but I don't see why you can't do cross-country.'

'Are you kidding?' He gave her an impatient look. 'Our school take it really seriously. Lots of the kids go on to run marathons. You can't do that if you have to stop to test your blood sugar all the time in case you're going hypo.'

'But what if you didn't have to stop?'

He stared at her. 'Well, of course, I have to stop.'

Ally shook her head slowly. 'They're bringing out new blood-glucose monitors all the time, you know, and there's one that's no bigger than a stopwatch so you can carry it with you when you run.'

'But I still have to stop—'

'No, you don't.' Ally racked her brains for the information the company representative had given her recently. 'You don't need test strips—it's all in the meter so you can test while you run.'

Pete's eyes were fixed on her face. 'Without even stopping?'

Ally nodded. 'That's right. Want me to find out more for you?'

'You bet!' Pete's eyes were shining. 'Wow, that would be great. Thanks, Dr McGuire.'

'No problem.' Ally glanced curiously at the pair of brand new climbing boots sitting on his locker. 'What are those?'

Pete coloured and looked proud. 'Oh, Dr Nicholson bought me those.'

Sean? He'd been to see Pete? Why hadn't he said?

Ally picked up the boots and turned them over in her hands. They were top quality and from one of the local climbing shops.

'He says if they don't fit I can change them when I'm on my feet again, but he never wants to catch me climbing in trainers again.' Pete's eyes glowed. 'And guess what? Dr Nicholson is going to give Andy and me some climbing lessons. Isn't that cool?'

Ally stared at him. 'Lessons?'

Pete nodded furiously. 'He was an instructor in the army, you know, and Mr Morgan says he's the best at climbing and abseiling and now he's going to teach us—isn't that brilliant?'

'Brilliant,' Ally echoed, fingering the boot thoughtfully. It wasn't what she would have expected of Sean. She'd thought he was cold and unemotional and certainly he hadn't shown any sympathy for the boys when he'd rescued them, but here he was not only buying an expensive pair of boots for Pete but also offering to give up his valuable time to give them climbing lessons. It didn't sound like the man she'd seen so far. Had she misjudged him?

'How many times has Dr Nicholson been in to see you?'

'Twice.' Pete watched as she placed the boots carefully back on the locker. 'He gave me a right rocket the first time. Told me I would have died if you and he hadn't been there—then he sat down and talked to me for ages. All about my diabetes and how I felt and stuff like that.'

Stuff like that. Stuff that really mattered to Pete. Ally bit her lip. Sean had done a good job by the look of it. She'd been expecting the boy to be really depressed, instead of which he was desperate to get better so that he could start his climbing lessons.

She spent a bit longer with Pete, teasing him and generally making him laugh, and then she glanced at her watch and grimaced.

'Oops, it's getting late.' She stood up and pulled on her coat. 'I've got to go, but I'll see you soon.'

Ally was pulling up outside the barn when the door of the stable opened and Sean strode out. Judging from the bag in his hand, he was going out on a call, and from the look on his face it was an emergency.

She touched the button for the electric window, shivering as the cold evening air oozed into the car. 'Problems?'

Sean glanced at his bike, hesitated and then strode towards her car, a decision made. He tugged open the passenger door and flung his bag in the footwell.

Ally immediately hit the accelerator. 'Where am I going?'

'Kelly Watson.'

'Oh, no!' Ally pulled out into the lane and drove as fast as she considered safe, her mind racing. 'Another asthma attack, I presume?'

'Yes, and a bad one from the sounds of it.' Sean fastened the seat belt in a fluid movement and glanced quickly at his watch. 'They tried to call an ambulance but there's been a pile-up on the motorway so there was no chance of anything arriving quickly. Her mother's in a total panic.'

Knowing Kelly's mother, Ally could well imagine it. Thank goodness she knew exactly where they lived.

Less than five minutes later she braked outside a row of cottages and jerked her head towards the one on the end.

'That's the house.'

Sean was out of the car in a flash, muttering something under his breath as he saw Kelly's mother hovering anxiously by the front door.

'Thank goodness you've come!' Mrs Watson's face was streaked with tears and she hurried through to the sitting room. 'She's in here, but she can hardly breathe...'

Sean strode through the door and Ally gave Mrs Watson's arm a squeeze. 'Try and clam down if you can or you'll panic Kelly.'

Mrs Watson gave a huge gulp. 'Don't let her die, Dr McGuire—please, don't let her die—'

'She won't die,' Ally said firmly, and gave her a gentle push in the direction of the kitchen. 'How about putting the kettle on?'

Not that she wanted any tea, but she knew that they'd need to assess the situation without an agitated mother peering over their shoulders.

Kelly was lying on the sofa, struggling for breath, a bluish tinge colouring her lips.

Sean's hands were already in his bag, drawing up salbutamol. 'She needs high-flow oxygen.'

Ally was ahead of him, handing him the mask and tubing even as he finished saying the words.

'I'm going to use aminophylline.'

Ally delved into his case and pulled out the ampoule. 'How much does Kelly weigh, Mrs Watson?'

There was a brief silence. 'About four stone.'

Sean pulled a face. 'What the hell's that in kilograms?'

Ally did a quick mental calculation even as he was drawing up the drug. 'Say 25 kilos.'

Sean cast an eye over the little girl. 'Sounds about right. OK, so I'll give her 5 milligrams per kilo.'

'One twenty-five milligrams,' Ally agreed, taking the little girl's hand and giving it a squeeze. 'You're doing fine, Kelly. You'll soon be breathing easier, sweetheart.'

Kelly just looked at her, her eyes dull and exhausted, too short of breath to even attempt to speak.

'Let's give her some hydrocortisone as well,' Ally murmured, and Sean nodded.

'She's got severe bronchospasm. We might need to bag and mask her.'

Ally met his eyes briefly and then delved into the case for

the equipment they might need. Kelly's breathing was more and more laboured, and Ally glanced up and caught Mrs Watson standing in the doorway, her face white and pinched.

'She's breathing more easily—her respirations are down slightly,' Sean murmured suddenly, settling the mask more comfortably on the little girl's face.

'Thank goodness for that.' Ally stood up, wincing as her cramped muscles protested violently.

Mrs Watson glanced out through the window. 'The ambulance is here.'

Sean nodded briefly and adjusted the mask. 'Right. Well, she still needs to go to hospital. She's better, no doubt about that, but her colour and her breathing could still improve a lot so let's get her loaded into that ambulance.'

Ally smiled at the paramedic who strode into the room. 'Hi, Daniel. Things are looking a little better here but we still need your help.'

'Will do.' He stared down at the little girl and gave her a wink. 'Can't stay away from me, can you, pet? I was here last week, wasn't I?'

Kelly managed a weak smile and Daniel sat next to her and soothed her gently while Ally gave a brief but thorough description of what had happened and the treatment they'd given.

Daniel stood up as his partner came in with a chair covered in red blankets. 'One of you coming in the ambulance?'

Sean frowned. 'I'm still on call…'

'I'll go,' Ally said promptly, and then bit her lip. Charlie.

Sean scanned her face and held out his hand. 'Give me your keys and I'll be in when Charlie comes home. If I get a call, Charlie can come with me.'

Ally hesitated. 'My mum can probably stay with her…' But, then again, maybe not. She'd told her mother that she'd be home so she might have made plans. The farm kept her whole family busy. She didn't have a choice. Delving into her bag, she handed Sean the keys and then followed Daniel out to the ambulance, helping to settle Kelly comfortably while Mrs Watson locked the house.

As the ambulance pulled away Ally gave the woman a comforting smile. 'She'll be just fine now, Mrs Watson.'

'Until the next time.'

Ally nodded slowly. 'Yes, well, we need to get to the bottom of this. I'll talk to the hospital when they've had a chance to assess her. It is unusual that she wasn't better controlled on that dose of steroids she's been taking.'

Was it her imagination or was Mrs Watson avoiding looking at her? Her instincts told her that something wasn't quite right...

'How long will she have to stay in?' Mrs Watson rummaged in her bag for a tissue and blew her nose hard.

'She'll probably be allowed home tomorrow,' Ally told her, steadying herself as the ambulance went round a corner. 'Do you have any idea what triggered this attack, Mrs Watson? Has she been in contact with animals or anything different that might have caused it?'

Was there the briefest hesitation?

'I don't know.' Mrs Watson shook her head firmly.

'Right.' Ally watched her carefully. 'Well, we'll have to think about it.'

Lucy's words about Kelly's mother not being keen on drugs came back to her, and she frowned briefly. Was that what was happening? Was she withholding the drugs? She made a mental note to follow it up as soon as Kelly was out of hospital.

Ally heard the laughter as soon as she pushed open the door of the barn.

Charlie was lying on her stomach on the big rug in front of the fire, her legs swinging from left to right, and Sean was sprawled across from her in the process of loading small white balls into a tunnel.

'Hi, Mum!' Charlie grinned delightedly. 'We're playing Hungry Hippos. I've won twice.'

'She's violent,' Sean murmured wryly, smacking Charlie's hand gently as she leaned across to steal a ball. 'That's mine, you cheat!'

Charlie giggled furiously and then pounded the plastic hippo with her hand until it swallowed the ball.

'I've won another one!' she whooped, and wriggled into a sitting position, her blonde hair awry as she beamed at Sean.

Ally dropped her bag and sank onto one of the squishy white sofas which had been her biggest indulgence. 'So, how was the party, tuppence?'

'Oh, great! There were some brilliant costumes but mine was the brilliantest.'

'The most brilliant,' Ally corrected automatically.

'My mask was scary, wasn't it, Sean?'

'Terrifying.' Sean's eyes gleamed and swivelled to Ally who was feeling thoroughly agitated. Whatever she'd been expecting, it certainly hadn't been a cosy domestic scene, with Sean playing with her daughter. Somehow she'd thought he'd be reading quietly on one of her sofas while Charlie played in her bedroom—instead of which he was lying on his side on her rug, his jeans clinging to the hard muscle of his thighs, a glimpse of dark hair showing on his chest as his shirt buttons gaped slightly. He looked devastatingly male and thoroughly at home.

Surely he'd said he didn't like children...

She bit her lip and dragged her gaze away from the question she saw in his.

'Dr Nicholson has got to go now, darling, so finish the game quickly.'

Sean watched her, one eyebrow lifting, and she felt thoroughly flustered. What was he thinking?

Suddenly he gave a soft smile. 'I'm not in a hurry.'

Damn the man! His dark eyes teased her gently and she swallowed hard. He knew she wanted him to go but he wasn't going to take the hint.

'Can't he stay to supper?' Charlie bounced onto the sofa next to her mother and crossed her legs. 'I could dress up again and scare you.'

'No, thanks, you might give me nightmares.' A wicked glint appeared in his eyes as they met Ally's. 'And I'm having enough trouble sleeping as it is.'

Ally coloured and got up quickly to hide her embarrassment. No way was this man staying to supper. She'd choke!

'How was Kelly?' He rose in one fluid movement and suddenly he was standing right next to her, tall, well muscled and very, very male.

'Fine. Much better.' Why wouldn't he stop looking at her? It made her feel peculiar...

'Can't Sean stay to supper, Mum?' Charlie wheedled, and Ally gave Sean a threatening look.

'You're much too busy this evening, aren't you, Sean?'

'Me?' He raised his eyebrows and smiled innocently. 'Not unless my bleeper goes off. I'd love to stay to supper.'

'Yippee!' Charlie leapt off the sofa and charged into her bedroom, leaving Ally grinding her teeth in frustration.

Sean gave a low laugh and dropped onto the sofa. 'It was kind of you to invite me.'

Damn the man! Ally took a deep breath and struggled with her temper. 'I did not invite you! I don't want you to stay to supper and you know it!'

'Why?' The sharp question and the look in his eyes made her heart stumble.

'Because I've already told you I don't want you getting close to Charlie.'

He raised an eyebrow and stretched out those long legs. 'Close to Charlie or close to you?'

'Neither.' She stared at him fiercely, her chest rising and falling as she breathed. 'Please, Sean...'

He rose suddenly, catching her arm in a firm grip when she would have backed away.

'Oh, no, you don't. Not until we've talked about this.' His

fingers bit into her forearm as he pulled her back towards him. 'Are you still trying to say there's no chemistry between us?'

There was a long silence as they stared at each other and then she sagged slightly.

'No.' She stood still, her breathing irregular. 'No, I'm not saying that.'

His expression softened slightly and he brushed her cheek with gentle fingers. 'Then why won't you just let things take their course?'

'Because it isn't worth the pain you'll cause Charlie and me,' she said bleakly, trying without success to pull away from him. 'It just isn't worth it.'

He stared down at her for a long moment, a muscle working in his jaw, and then his head came down and his mouth captured hers, his kiss hot and demanding.

She gave a gasp of shock and tried to pull away, but long, strong fingers clamped the back of her head, preventing her escape, while his other arm slid down her back and pulled her firmly against him.

It was a kiss like no other she'd ever received—fiery, erotic, gentle and demanding all at the same time—and soon she forgot that she'd ever wanted to escape. All she wanted was more. His touch was totally addictive and, instead of pulling away, she leaned against him, feeling the hard muscle of his thighs pressing against her, wanting to feel every male inch of him against her.

The hand behind her head tightened and he made love to her mouth with a skill and expertise that left every feminine nerve ending in her body crying out for more.

Tentatively her hand travelled up to his neck touching the surprisingly soft hair at the back of his head, her heart pounding as his tongue danced with hers, dominating but at the same time gentle, encouraging her more timid response.

Her senses whirling, her free hand lifted to his chest, feeling the solid strength of muscle under the thin fabric of his shirt, feeling the steady thud of his heart. Ally could think of nothing but the way he made her feel. The way no one had ever made her feel before...

Sean growled something inarticulate and then dragged his mouth away from hers, trailing hot, biting kisses down the length of her throat before cupping her face in his hands.

His breathing was harsh and uneven as he stared down at her. 'Now tell me it's not worth it, Ally.'

And with that he released her and turned on his heel, leaving her with limbs trembling and heart pounding, wondering what had hit her.

CHAPTER FIVE

ALLY closed the door of her consulting room and sank into her chair. She couldn't concentrate on the flickering computer screen in front of her. She couldn't concentrate on the list of patients waiting to be seen or the mountain of results to be checked. In fact, she couldn't concentrate on anything. It was a cold Monday morning and all she could think about was Sean and the way it had felt when he'd kissed her.

Why had she let him do that? Why?

She gave a groan and closed her eyes. The truth was that he hadn't given her any choice. At least not in the beginning. But after that...well, after that she'd been as keen as him. Something had sparked between them, something she'd never known could happen.

She opened her eyes and lifted her chin. Well, it wasn't going to happen again. It was only a kiss, for goodness' sake. She could live with a kiss.

Straightening in her chair, she bit her lip, her emotions tumbled. How was she going to face him? He hadn't stayed to supper on Saturday night. He hadn't even stayed to have a conversation. He'd just kissed her until she'd been a gibbering wreck and then had walked out, leaving her to deal with the aftermath of her unleashed emotions. And now she had to face him.

Pulling herself together, she picked up the stack of results on her desk and started going through them, noting which were fine and which needed follow-up.

A tap on her door made her jump, and her hands trembled as the door opened and Sean strode in, closing the door firmly behind him.

Ally stared at him warily and he gave her a wry smile.

'Don't look like that. I've come to apologise.'

'What for? Forcing me to kiss you? Taking over my home?' Ruining a perfectly peaceful existence by making her feel things she didn't know it was possible to feel? She glared at him, anger masking the other emotions that wrestled inside her.

He gave a short laugh and raked long fingers through his cropped hair. 'Like I said, I'm sorry. I suppose I'm just not very good at taking no for an answer.'

'Well, you'd better learn fast because it's the only answer you're ever going to get.' Ally turned back to her pile of results, determined that he wouldn't see how much her hands were shaking.

'Why?' His voice was hoarse and heart-stoppingly male. 'Because you want to protect Charlie? Maybe she doesn't need protecting. People come and go all the time—it's a fact of life.'

'Not for everyone.' Ally stared at the results without seeing them. 'Some people are lucky enough to have constancy and permanent relationships, and that's what I want for Charlie. I don't want her hurt.'

He paced over to the window, the tension visible in those broad shoulders as he stared out across the fells. 'So you refuse to take any risks or have any fun of your own in case it ends up hurting Charlie.'

'And me.' Ally stared bleakly at his broad back. 'In case it ends up hurting me. Which is what you'd do, Sean.'

He turned then, his dark eyes intense. 'You don't know that.'

She knew that. Dear God, she knew. 'You'd break my heart, Sean—'

'This is totally illogical.' He raked long fingers through his hair and made an impatient sound. 'What is it you want? Guarantees? There are never any guarantees—people never start a relationship knowing how's it going to end.'

'You do. You've told me as much.' She held his gaze steadily. 'You're very honest about the fact that you avoid intimacy and you don't want children, so a relationship with you can only have one ending—and it's not the one I want.'

He stared at her for a long moment, his jaw tense. 'There are reasons for the way I feel.'

'Share them.'

There was a rap on the door and Helen entered with a pile of notes, smiling briefly as she noticed Sean.

'Oh, hello, there, Dr Nicholson. I didn't know you were in here.'

To his credit, Sean managed a fairly genuine smile. Ally was ready to scream at the practice manager for her lousy timing. Sean had been about to open up to her, she was sure of it, but instead he glanced at his watch and gave Ally a brief nod that reflected none of the intimacy of their conversation only seconds earlier.

'I'd better get on. I've got patients to see.'

And with that he strode out, leaving Ally in a worse state than she'd been in when he'd entered the room ten minutes before.

Helen discussed a few problems with her and then left, leaving Ally to pull herself together before the stream of patients started.

Her first patient was Jenny Monroe, looking white and strained, a small bandage visible under her tights.

'Hello, Jenny.' Ally pushed her own problem to one side. 'I gather you managed to get an appointment very quickly?'

Jenny nodded. 'They rang me the day after because they had a cancellation. I had it taken out, but they said they think it's malignant. I have to go back on Thursday for the results.'

'I'm sorry, Jenny.' Ally felt a rush of sympathy for the young woman. Why was life so unfair? Jenny was so young and the diagnosis of malignant melanoma was a serious one.

'They said that they'd have to measure the thickness of the mole and that will give them an idea of how serious it is.' Jenny looked sick and suddenly burst into tears. 'I just keep thinking I'm going to die.'

'You mustn't think that!' Ally said firmly. 'You don't have

all the facts yet, and when you do we'll just make sure you have the very best treatment. You aren't going to die, Jenny.'

Jenny sniffed and took the tissue Ally offered her. 'Thanks. I suppose I'm just being stupid. People do survive cancer, don't they, even if they're told they're not going to?'

'They do, indeed. Positive thinking is terribly important in fighting any illness, Jenny,' Ally agreed, 'but you haven't been told any of those things—you're just letting your imagination run away with you. With luck it will have been caught in the very early stages—you'll probably just need regular checks.'

'I read in a magazine about using interferon for skin cancer—would I be suitable for that?'

Ally blinked. Nowadays patients were so much better informed than they used to be, and it was always quite tough on the GP who had to be three steps ahead of what was being printed in the press.

'Skin cancers haven't generally responded well to chemotherapy, but you're right that alpha interferon has shown some very promising results. I'm not sure exactly which patients it's suitable for but when we have more details from the hospital we can ask the consultant. You could ask them at your next appointment. It's important that you understand the treatment they're recommending.'

Jenny bit her lip. 'I can't, Dr McGuire. Once they start talking about cancer I know I'll just clam up. I hear that one word and then I don't hear anything else.'

Ally leaned forward and gave her hand a squeeze. 'Well, that's why it's a good idea to take someone with you. Can your husband take time off?'

'He has to look after the twins. My mother's away...' Jenny's eyes filled again and Ally reached for the phone, tapping in a number and then covering the receiver while she talked to Jenny.

'When's the appointment?'

'Thursday at four o'clock.'

Ally uncovered the receiver and waited. 'Mum? It's me. I need a favour.'

She listened and smiled while her mother made the usual remarks and then her face sobered. 'Could you babysit two eight-month-old twins for an hour while their mother goes to hospital for an appointment?' She talked for a few minutes more then replaced the receiver and scribbled her address on a piece of paper.

'This is where I live. My daughter Charlie is five and my mother will be looking after her until I finish evening surgery, so you're welcome to drop your two off on your way to the hospital. That way you get time to concentrate on what's being said and what you want to ask.'

Jenny took the piece of paper and gazed at it, her expression slightly stunned. 'Are you sure...?'

'Absolutely.' Ally gave her a gentle smile. 'And if you still don't feel you've asked all the questions you want to ask, I'll have a word with Mr Gordon.'

'Bless you, Dr McGuire.' Jenny tucked the paper safely inside her purse and blew her nose loudly. 'I'll probably be OK once I know what's going on. It's just the uncertainty that gets to me, you know?'

Ally nodded sympathetically. 'It must be very tough, but try and stay positive. The other people you might find useful to get in touch with are the support group CancerBACUP. They're in London but they have a helpline, with trained nurses giving information and answering all sorts of questions which you might not want to ask the doctor.'

She flicked through her address files and scribbled down another number which she handed to Jenny.

'Now then, I'll tell Mum to expect you on Thursday, and in the meantime give me a ring if you're really fretting about anything.'

Jenny stood up and smiled, looking much more relaxed. 'I can't thank you enough...'

'Nothing to thank me for,' Ally said gruffly, standing up, too, and walking to the door with her. 'I'll see you soon.'

She watched Jenny go and sent up a silent prayer that the tumour would have been caught early or, better still, be benign.

The rest of the week was a busy one with the beginnings of a flu outbreak which kept her and the partners busy.

Ally collapsed into a chair in the staffroom with a groan after one particularly busy morning.

'My muscles ache.'

'Flu?' suggested Lucy helpfully, handing her a mug of coffee and reaching for the biscuits.

'I hope not!' Ally took the coffee but waved aside the biscuits. 'I can't afford to be ill. I'm the doctor.'

'Well, you'd better wear a mask, then,' Lucy suggested cheerfully, 'because everyone I've seen this morning is brewing something hideous.'

'Oh, thanks!' The phone buzzed and Ally reached across to answer it, all her senses suddenly on alert as she saw Sean walk in. 'Hello?'

She listened for a moment and then reached for a pen and a pad. 'Yes, she's my patient. Fire away.' She scribbled for a minute and then gave a grin. 'Brilliant. Thanks a lot... Yes, I'll tell her.'

She replaced the receiver and smiled at Lucy. 'That was the lab. Felicity Webster has immunity to chickenpox so that's one worry gone.'

'Oh, that's good.' Lucy smiled and snuggled into a chair, folding her legs under her. 'I saw her in Sainsbury's last night. She looked as though she was about to deliver any moment. When's she due?'

'Not for another two weeks.'

Lucy shook her head slowly. 'No way is that woman going to last two weeks. She'll have delivered by Saturday if you ask me.'

'Clairvoyant, Lucy?' Sean dropped into a chair next to her and stretched out his long legs.

Lucy yawned. 'No. I just know when a woman's about to deliver.'

Ally laughed. 'You should go and work in the obstetric unit, then they could throw away the ultrasound. Are you all right? You look exhausted.'

'I am.' Lucy rubbed her eyes and stifled another yawn. 'I'm spending every spare minute training. Red and I have got our assessment coming up in a while.'

Sean raised an eyebrow. 'Who's Red?'

'Red's my Border collie,' Lucy told him proudly. 'We've been training for search and rescue so that we can join the mountain rescue team. If we pass we can go on call-outs. Talking of which, are you two going to the fireworks on Saturday?'

Lucy glanced at them and Ally couldn't hide her blush. She wished people wouldn't keep addressing them as a couple. Will, Jack and now Lucy.

'We are, indeed.' Sean's eyes held hers for a long moment. 'I promised Charlie.'

He'd promised Charlie? When had he promised Charlie? She'd known he'd be there, of course, but that didn't mean they had to go together.

'I've promised to help with the food for my sins.' Lucy chatted away happily, oblivious to the tension simmering in the room. 'Jack's selling tickets for five pounds. Jolly good idea really. Just baked potatoes and things like that.'

Ally dragged her gaze away from Sean's and managed a smile. 'Super. Just the thing for a cold night.'

Excusing herself, she made her way to her consulting room, relieved that she had a busy surgery to take her mind off Sean.

The first patient she saw was Mary Thompson, looking as anxious as ever.

'Hello, Mrs Thompson,' Ally greeted her warmly. 'How's that cough?'

'Cough?' For a moment the woman looked baffled and then she shook herself and gave a weak smile. 'Oh, that. Yes, well, it hasn't bothered me really...'

'Good. So what can I help you with today.'

Mary fingered her coat nervously. 'It's difficult...'

Ally leaned forward and covered her hand with her own. 'Mrs Thompson, I know something is wrong—why don't you trust me and just tell me what it is?'

Mary shook her head and then burst into tears. Ally handed her some tissues and waited for the storm to pass.

'I'm sorry about that, Doctor.' The woman sniffed and blew her nose. 'I'm just being a silly woman.'

'Tell me,' Ally prompted gently, and Mary took a deep breath.

'It's my husband. He's got a bit of a problem.'

Ally suspected that that was an understatement but she didn't speak, just waited for Mary to finish.

'It started when he took this job. Too much entertaining, sales conferences and targets which he couldn't meet.' She gave a sigh and stared helplessly at Ally. 'He's drinking. A lot. I suppose you saw the newspaper article.'

Ally hesitated and then nodded. There was no point in lying. 'Yes. Yes, I did, actually.'

'Frankly, I'm amazed it hasn't happened before.' Mary crumpled the tissue into a ball and fiddled nervously with it. 'He's been drinking far too much for at least a year.'

And driving. Ally gritted her teeth and tried not to think about the damage he could have done.

'Will he come in and see me, Mrs Thompson?'

The older woman shrugged her shoulders and gave her a bleak look. 'Well, before that newspaper article I would have said no. He's a very proud man. Very traditional, you know? Won't ever admit he needs help. But now—well, to be frank, he just might because he feels so down. I've been trying to persuade him to come and see you. I did wonder whether there was anything I could do...'

Ally shook her head. 'Not really, Mrs Thompson. If he's drinking as much as you say then he needs professional help now. We need to check his current state of health—see what damage the alcohol has done—and then break the addiction. The best thing you can do is get him to come and see me. He has to want to change things or a detoxification programme has no chance of working.'

The woman slumped in the chair and sighed. 'It's all so complicated.'

'Has he hurt you at all, Mrs Thompson?' Ally asked gently. 'Does he get violent when he's drunk?'

'No. That's one thing I should be grateful for, I suppose.'

'Try and get him to come and see me,' Ally said as the woman stood up to leave. 'I'm sure we can help him.'

She watched as Mary walked down the corridor, her figure bent and defeated. Ally frowned. She'd have a word with Will and see if he had any bright ideas how to persuade Mr Thompson to come and see her.

Charlie was baking biscuits in the kitchen with her grandmother when Ally arrived home. She dropped her bag and pushed open the kitchen door, sniffing in appreciation. 'Mmm. Something smells good.' She stopped dead as she saw Sean lounging comfortably at the kitchen table, laughing with her mother. What was he doing here?

'Hello, pet.' Her mother was in the process of wiping flour from the kitchen table. 'We're just stocking up the freezer, aren't we, Charlie?'

'Yup.' Charlie grinned, her sweet face covered in tell-tale signs of cake mixture.

'We've made an orange one for us and two chocolate ones for Uncle Jack's firework party.'

'I told Jack I'd donate two and if he wanted any more he'd have to buy them,' her mother said cheerfully. 'We're so busy on the farm at the moment I haven't got time to cook. I've made you a casserole and I made sure there's enough for Sean, too. I thought it would be nice if he joined you.'

Ally gaped at her mother who beamed at her.

Sean unfolded his length from the chair and gave her mother a gracious smile. 'That's very kind of you, Mrs McGuire. I'll just nip next door and get a bottle of wine,' he said smoothly, his eyes gleaming with humour as he scanned the look on Ally's face.

The minute he'd gone Ally sent Charlie off to find a book and rounded on her mother. 'What are you playing at, Mum?'

Her mother turned the last of the sponge cakes onto a wire rack to cool. 'Inviting that gorgeous man to join you for dinner.'

Ally was appalled. 'But I don't want to eat dinner with him!'

'Then you need your head examined,' her mother said calmly, dropping the dirty cake tins into the sink and putting water on them to soak. 'He's handsome, intelligent and single, and if I weren't still in love with your father I'd be eating dinner with him myself.'

Ally shrugged off her coat. 'I can't believe I'm hearing this. You're pairing me up with someone you met five minutes ago? You don't know anything about him!'

Elaine McGuire stilled, a slight frown touching her fine, elegant features. 'Oh, yes, I do. I know a great deal about him. I've known Sean Nicholson since he was three years old.'

Ally gaped at her and dropped into a chair. 'You've known—? Mum! How? How come I don't remember him, then?'

Her mother shrugged. 'He's quite a bit older than you…'

'Did you know his parents?'

'No.' Watching her mother's face tighten, Ally felt a sense of foreboding. 'He was abandoned by his mother when he was two.'

Ally's eyes widened in shock. Abandoned? Sean had been abandoned by his own mother? What sort of a woman would do a thing like that? Suddenly her limbs felt shaky and she was glad she was sitting down. She didn't know what she'd expected but it certainly hadn't been that.

'What about his dad?'

'Goodness knows. I don't think his mother even knew who the father was.' Elaine frowned. 'I probably shouldn't even be telling you this, but it's pretty common knowledge really. He was in and out of foster-care for his entire childhood—probably would have got into real trouble if it hadn't been for Will and Molly.'

'What did they do?' Everything was starting to fall into place. The way he felt so strongly that children should have two parents. His fear of commitment.

'Well, eventually they gave him a home, of course, but it was more than that.' Her mother wiped her hands on her apron. 'Will got him involved in the outdoor pursuits centre, which was where he met Jack. Sean helped out in return for tuition and then he joined the army and no one really heard of him after that. I never imagined he'd become a doctor, but obviously living with the Carters must have rubbed off.'

'He's a brilliant doctor,' Ally mumbled, thinking about all the times she'd seen him in action. Totally cool and controlled and yet capable of sensitivity, too—after all, look how he'd been with Pete.

'Yes, I can imagine he would be.' Her mother looked at her thoughtfully. 'He was considered quite brilliant as a boy but too lazy and quick with his fists to spend time bothering with his brain.'

Ally shook her head slowly. 'But why hasn't Will ever mentioned him?'

Her mother shrugged. 'The Carters fostered quite a few children and I don't think Sean was the best at keeping in touch.'

He'd admitted as much himself. Ally fiddled idly with some cake crumbs. 'And he won't be around for long this time either. He's just helping Will out—says he owes him a favour.'

'I expect he does.' Her mother dried the cake tins and laid

them carefully on the table. 'And if he's not going to be here for long, you'd better make the most of him while you can.'

Ally gasped. 'Mum!'

'What?' Elaine gave a sigh. 'Ally, I would have to be both blind and stupid not to have picked up the vibes between the two of you. It's never really bothered me before, you putting your life on hold for Charlie, because I knew you'd never met a man worthy of you anyway, but if you let this opportunity slip through your fingers then you'll regret it.'

'But he doesn't want commitment and he says he never wants children.'

'Well, we all say things we don't mean,' her mother replied calmly. 'Would you want children and commitment after all he went through as a child?'

'Probably not.' Ally cast her mind back to his comments about people who became parents. If he'd suffered so much abandonment in his life, no wonder he shied away from forging relationships. 'But what happens when he moves on?'

'Then you have your memories,' her mother said crisply. 'Better a brief relationship with Mr Right than a lifetime with Mr Wrong, don't you think? I know you're thinking of Rob and Paul, but don't—they weren't worth ruining your life over.'

Ally stared at her. 'But there's Charlie…'

'You've always done the right thing by Charlie but she's not made of glass, sweetheart.' Elaine checked that the cakes were cool and then wrapped them up in clingfilm. 'Thanks to you, she's more than capable of coping with a few knocks in life. Now, I'm late and your dad will be worrying so I'm going to make a move.'

She stooped and kissed her daughter and picked up her coat on her way out, leaving Ally sitting at the table lost in thought. She was still there when Sean returned ten minutes later, bottle in hand.

'Has your mum gone?'

'What?' Ally blinked and managed a shaky smile. 'Oh—yes.

She had to drop two chocolate cakes off with Jack on the way home.'

Sean frowned and set the bottle down on the table, reaching for a corkscrew. 'Are you all right?'

'Fine.' Ally stood up and checked the casserole, removing the lid and giving it a stir.

'Don't tell me—your mother told you that I was a bad influence and that you should run a mile.'

Ally gave a short laugh and tossed the spoon into the washing-up bowl, before opening a cupboard and handing him two glasses. She watched while he poured the amber liquid and handed her a glass.

'On the contrary, she was recommending that I jump into bed with you at the earliest possible moment.'

There was a moment's stunned silence and then Sean threw back his head and laughed, a rich, totally male sound that made her nerve endings tingle.

'Was she now? Well, I never—what a fantastic woman.'

'She remembered you...'

The smile faded and those dark eyes narrowed. 'Ah, now I see. She doubtless regaled you with harrowing tales of my depraved youth.'

She blushed under the heavy sarcasm and took a sip of wine. 'Well, let's just say I can now understand why you avoid commitment.'

His jaw tightened. 'I see.'

Something about his chilly tone made her hesitate. 'Well, it can't have been easy for you—'

'Spare me the psychology, Ally. I don't need it!' All traces of warmth had vanished and his eyes glittered angrily. 'So what have you decided? That you'll let me have my wicked way with you because you feel sorry for me?'

Ally frowned. Boy, was he sensitive about his past! 'Don't be ridiculous...'

His mouth was a grim line. 'Don't patronise me, Ally! I can see it in your face. All of a sudden I'm a poor boy who needs

PLAY BANGO! AND GET FIVE FREE GIFTS!

It looks like BINGO, it plays like BINGO but it's FREE!
HOW TO PLAY:

1. With a coin, scratch the Caller Card to reveal your 5 lucky numbers and see whether they match your Bango Card. Then check the claim chart to discover what we have for you — up to 4 FREE BOOKS and a FREE GIFT — ALL YOURS, ALL FREE!

2. Send back the Bango card and you'll receive free Mills & Boon® Medical Romance™ books. These books have a cover price of £2.40 each, but they are yours to keep absolutely free.

3. There's no catch. You're under no obligation to buy anything. We charge nothing — ZERO — for your first shipment. And you don't have to make any minimum number of purchases — not even one!

4. The fact is, thousands of readers enjoy receiving our books by post from the Reader Service™. They like the convenience of home delivery and they like getting the best new novels before they are available in the shops. And of course, postage and packing is COMPLETELY FREE!

5. We hope that after receiving your free books you'll want to remain a subscriber. But the choice is yours — to continue or cancel any time! So why not take us up on our invitation, with no risk of any kind you'll be glad you did!

YOURS FREE!
This exciting mystery gift is yours free when you play BANGO!

It's fun, and we're giving away
FREE GIFTS
to all players!

PLAY BANGO!

CALLER CARD

SCRATCH HERE!

YES!
Please send me the gifts for which I qualify! I understand that I am under no obligation to purchase any books as explained on the back of this card.

YOUR CARD ↴

BANGO

38	9	44	10	38
92	7	5	27	14
2	51	FREE	91	67
75	3	12	20	13
6	15	26	50	31

CLAIM CHART!

Match 5 numbers	4 FREE BOOKS & A MYSTERY GIFT
Match 4 numbers	2 FREE BOOKS & A MYSTERY GIFT
Match 3 numbers	2 FREE BOOKS

M1AI

Ms/Mrs/Miss/Mr _____ Initials _____
BLOCK CAPITALS PLEASE
Surname _____
Address _____
_____
Postcode _____

Offer valid in the UK only and is not available to current Reader Service subscribers to this series. Overseas and Eire please write for details. We reserve the right to refuse an application and applicants must be aged 18 years or over. Only one application per household. Offer expires 31st July 2001. Terms and prices are subject to change without notice. As a result of this application you may receive further offers from other carefully selected companies. If you do not wish to share in this opportunity, please write to the Data Manager at the address shown overleaf.
Mills & Boon® is a registered trademark owned by Harlequin Mills & Boon Limited.
Medical Romance™ is being used as a trademark.

The Mills & Boon® Reader Service™ — Here's how it works:

Accepting your free books places you under no obligation to buy anything. You may keep the books and gift and return the despatch note marked "cancel." If you do not cancel, about a month later we'll send you 6 brand new books and invoice you for just £2.40* each. That's the complete price — there is no extra charge for postage and packing. You may cancel at anytime, otherwise, every month we'll send you 6 more books, which you may either purchase or return to us — the choice is yours.

*Terms and prices subject to change without notice.

MILLS & BOON READER SERVICE
FREE BOOK OFFER
FREEPOST CN81
CROYDON
CR9 3WZ

NO STAMP
NECESSARY
IF POSTED IN
THE U.K. OR N.I.

mothering and who'll change his ways for the love of a good woman.'

'I didn't say that—'

'You didn't have to.' He gave a wry smile and drained his wineglass in one gulp. 'Forget supper. All of a sudden I'm not hungry.' He banged his glass down on the table and strode out of the kitchen, leaving her staring, open-mouthed.

Ally tapped on the door of Sean's consulting room the next morning, taking a deep breath when she heard his clipped tone. He was working on the computer and his fingers stilled when she entered, his expression cool and unwelcoming.

'Yes?'

The words came out in a rush. 'I came to say I'm sorry. Mum wasn't gossiping, but I can see that it must have looked that way to you. And I don't feel sorry for you—at least, I suppose I do in a way but that hasn't got anything to do with me going to bed with you—' She broke off, horribly uncomfortable under his steady scrutiny.

He leaned back in his chair and raised an eyebrow. 'Are you telling me that you're sorry or that you want to go to bed with me?'

'Neither.' She blushed fiercely and chewed her lip. 'I mean, I am sorry, but— Oh damn you! You know what I mean.'

She glared at him and he stood up and walked across to her, his eyes suddenly gentle.

'And I'm sorry, too. I overreacted. I'm afraid my childhood isn't my favourite topic of conversation.' He lifted her chin and scanned her face. 'So, are you going to take your mother's advice?'

She looked away, her heart hammering. 'Don't tease me, Sean. It isn't fair.'

'Who's being fair?' He gave a short laugh and cupped her face in his hands, forcing her to look at him. 'It isn't fair that I have to look at you every day and not touch. It's no wonder

I'm behaving like a maimed lion. I'm suffering from a serious case of male frustration.'

'I don't parade myself!' Her mild protest was ignored and her stomach flipped over as he brushed his thumb along her lower lip.

'You're driving me nuts, do you know that?'

She was hypnotised by the look in his eyes and the husky tone of his voice. 'I'm not doing anything.'

'Exactly.' His smile was wry. 'I only have to think about what will happen when we finally make love and I'm a gibbering wreck.'

Her heart seemed to collide with her stomach and she shook her head and backed away from him. 'It won't happen, Sean.'

'It's got to—I need to start getting some sleep at night.' He gave her a rueful look that turned into a wicked grin. 'Mind you, that might not be the best way of ensuring sleep…'

She swallowed. 'You'd break my heart.'

He rubbed his forehead with long fingers and gave a short laugh. 'So you keep saying. I'm beginning to think you might have a similar effect on mine.'

'You haven't got a heart, Sean, remember?'

She opened the door and some little imp inside her made her lower her lashes, treating him to a teasing smile that made him catch his breath.

'Close the door and get yourself back in here.' His voice was a low growl but she merely widened the smile.

'I've got surgery, Dr Nicholson.'

And with that she waltzed out of the room, leaving Sean and temptation firmly behind her.

CHAPTER SIX

THE evening of the bonfire party was crisp and clear.

Ally put the final touches to her make-up and stared at herself critically in the mirror. She was wearing a thick, chunky sweater in a shade of blue that matched her eyes, and a pair of skin tight jeans tucked into soft suede boots. She frowned down at the boots. Would they get muddy? Probably not, she decided, remembering how bitterly cold the weather had been. The ground was likely to be as hard as rock. She lifted her hands to fasten her blonde hair on top of her head and then she hesitated, letting it fall softly around her shoulders. Oh, goodness, why not? A bonfire party in temperatures little above freezing was hardly the venue for natty dressing so the least she could allow herself was feminine-looking hair. Nothing to do with Sean, of course. Nothing at all.

Her heart gave a little jump as she sprayed on some perfume and grabbed her thick wool coat and scarf.

'Mum, come on!' Charlie's voice sailed up from the sitting room. 'Sean's here and we're going to be late.'

Ally took a steadying breath, flicked off the bedroom light and made her way down the spiral staircase that led directly to the living room.

Sean was waiting at the bottom, his powerful legs planted slightly apart, his shoulders looking wider than ever in the bulky jacket he'd chosen to wear. His eyes travelled slowly over her body, lingered on the golden hair fanned across her shoulders and settled on her face. For a brief moment his rakish dark eyes burned into hers and then he was turning his attention back to Charlie.

'Wow!' Charlie danced around at the bottom of the stairs,

her blonde hair tucked up inside a wool hat. 'You look like Cinderella with your hair like that, Mum—doesn't she, Sean?'

'She certainly does.' Sean's voice was husky and he shifted slightly as if he was suddenly uncomfortable. He caught her eye and his mouth twisted into a smile of wry self-mockery. 'I think we'd better go, don't you? I promised Jack we'd be there early enough to help out.'

'I love fireworks.' Charlie grabbed his hand and he swung her up into his arms.

'Come on, then, imp. Let's get you there.'

Holding her easily, he waited while Ally locked the door of the barn and followed her to the car. Ally stopped dead as she saw a brand new BMW parked next to her old Fiesta.

'What's that?'

Sean grinned. 'Your carriage, Cinderella. Let's just say I decided that a motorbike and a semi-rural GP practice in the middle of winter don't really go together.'

'It's fabulous.' Ally climbed inside and fingered the upholstery with awe. 'You lucky thing.'

'Surely you could afford a decent car if you wanted one?' Sean frowned across at her as he fastened his seat belt. 'I can't understand why you struggle so much financially. You must earn a reasonable salary.'

Ally's jaw set as she stared out of the window. She did. A very reasonable salary. But she also had debts. Debts she didn't want to explain to him.

'We're going to be late, Sean,' she said pointedly, and he stared at her for a moment and then gave a little shrug.

'None of my business. Fine.'

He released the handbrake and they drove to the park where the fireworks were being held.

There was a huge crowd there already and Charlie gasped when she saw the size of the bonfire.

'Oh, Mum, look! Can I go closer—please?'

Ally hesitated, naturally protective. 'Well, I don't know. You have to be careful, sweetheart—'

'I'll take her,' Sean said easily, swinging the little girl onto his shoulders and pacing across the field. Ally watched them go, trying to work out why she felt so anxious. Was it really because of the fire or was it because Sean was striking up such a good relationship with Charlie? Was this just another of his ploys to get close to her? Shaking off her worries, she made her way to the refreshment tent, smiling at people she knew and queuing up for some coffee. There was a slight commotion in the crowd of people just outside the tent and, peering out, she recognised Mary Thompson's husband, laughing loudly— too loudly. His wife was hovering anxiously at his elbow. Was he drunk?

Forgetting about the coffee, she pushed her way back outside. At first there were no signs of the Thompsons and then she heard raised voices and saw them on the edge of the field under some trees, obviously arguing. Geoff Thompson was shouting at his wife aggressively, and as she watched he raised his arm and hit Mary so hard that she staggered.

With a cry of outrage Ally sprinted across to them, giving no thought to what would happen when she got there. She just knew she had to stop him. As she ran up she saw that Mr Thompson was indeed very, very drunk.

'Just leave me alone and stop nagging, you stupid woman!' He rocked slightly on his feet and turned his head, bleary-eyed, as he noticed Ally for the first time. 'Wha' do you want?'

'Oh, Dr McGuire!' Mary covered her mouth with a hand to keep back the sobs which were shaking her body. Blood was pouring from a nasty cut on her head. 'Go away, please.'

'He hit you, Mary.' Ally's voice was controlled but her blood was boiling.

'And I'll hit you if you don't keep your nose out of it.' Mr Thompson stepped towards her, grabbing Ally by the jacket and giving her a rough push. She kept her balance—just—but now she was really angry.

'I don't advise it, Mr Thompson,' she said coldly, turning

her attention back to Mary. 'I need to have a look at that cut, Mary.'

'I said keep your nose out of it! Come any closer and you'll have more than a cut to worry about,' Mr Thompson growled, and stepped towards her again, his fists raised.

'Lay one finger on her and you won't be walking for a month.' The icy words came from behind her and Ally felt a surge of relief as she heard Sean's voice. 'Ally, get Mrs Thompson to the first-aid tent. I'll see you there in a minute.'

Without arguing, Ally slipped an arm round the woman's shoulders and glanced at Sean. There was something menacing about the hard set of his jaw and the glint in his eyes. Mr Thompson obviously thought so, too, because he started to bluster about it all being a big mistake.

'Sean, where's Charlie?'

He didn't turn. 'With Jack.'

Of course. She should have known he wouldn't bring her daughter into danger. She hurried Mary towards the tent and settled her in a chair. One of the St John's Ambulance crew came across and offered sympathy while Ally assessed the damage. Fortunately the cut was fairly superficial.

'This looks much worse than it is, Mary. Scalps always bleed a lot, but it doesn't need stitches. I'll just put some paper strips across it but you're going to have a glorious black eye.'

She delved into the first-aid kit proffered by her uniformed helper just as Sean strode into the tent. His face was grim.

'How is she?'

Ally shrugged. 'The physical damage is fairly superficial but as for the rest…'

Sean gave a brief nod. 'In that case, I want a quick word outside.'

Ally looked surprised but finished dressing the cut and rose to her feet, giving Mary a quick pat on the hand. 'Mary, do you have somewhere to stay tonight? I think you'd better leave Geoff to sober up and then we can work out what we're going to do about him.'

'I have a friend who will let me stay with her,' said Mary quietly, 'but the only one who can do anything about Geoff is himself. I've tried my best…'

'Then hopefully, this night spent without you will make him see what he is in danger of losing,' Ally squeezed her hand. 'Stay here for a while, and someone will contact your friend for you. There will be a solution, Mary, believe me.'

Mary gave a small shake of her head and accepted the tea that the St John's Ambulance woman was offering her.

Outside the tent Ally turned to look at the bonfire, anxious about Charlie, but Sean planted a hand on her shoulder and dragged her round to face him.

'What the hell were you playing at?'

She stared into the naked fury in his dark eyes and frowned as his strong fingers bit into her shoulders. 'What do you mean?'

'What do I mean?' He stared at her incredulously and gave her a little shake. 'For goodness' sake, woman, do I have to spell it out? A drunken man has a go at his wife and you intervene.'

'And?'

His mouth tightened. 'And it could have been you next.'

She frowned. 'Well, I was glad to see you, that's for sure—thanks for that, Sean.'

He released her with a sigh of frustration and dragged both hands through his hair. 'You just don't get it, do you? You could have been seriously hurt, but if there's something you want to do then you just do it, don't you, no matter how many people might be worrying about you?'

'Hold on.' She stared at him, her irritation mounting. 'You're saying I should have stood back and let him wallop her?'

'If necessary.' Sean gritted his teeth. 'You could have called for me or Jack or the police—anything rather than just wading in yourself. It was just luck that I saw what was going on.'

'Well, I didn't have time for that—he was hitting her, for

goodness' sake!' Her eyes blazed angrily and he gave a short, humourless laugh.

'I noticed—and you were going to be next! You're going to get yourself in serious trouble one day. You just don't seem to think about your personal safety—you wade in and intervene with a drunk man three times your size, you walk in the fells on your own—'

Ally made an impatient sound. 'Oh, not that again!'

'You have a five-year-old daughter relying on you—it's totally irresponsible!'

She gasped and curled her fingers into her palms. 'How dare you, you—you—hypocrite? How dare you lecture me about responsibility when you won't take any yourself. You flit through life just having a good time, giving no thought to anyone else and moving on when it suits you, and you dare talk to me about responsibility.'

How could she ever have found this man so attractive? Did she have no common sense at all? She ought to tell him to take a running jump. 'I'm very aware of my responsibilities to Charlie. It's one of the reasons I'm not jumping into bed with you—remember?!'

With that she spun on her heel and stormed off across the grass, tears burning behind her eyes. She wasn't going to cry. No way. She wouldn't give him the satisfaction of knowing he was capable of hurting her. How dared he criticise her when she'd only been trying to help? He was totally insufferable and high-handed, thinking that only a man can handle certain situations, implying that she hadn't spared a thought for Charlie.

In the distance she saw Jack and walked towards him with relief—someone to take her mind off Sean. Fortunately most of the crowd were near the bonfire so they wouldn't have heard the angry exchange of words.

Will and his wife, Molly, were chatting to Jack when she arrived, and Charlie was leaping up and down like a grasshopper.

'Mum, Mum!' She was dancing on the spot, pink-cheeked

from cold and excitement. 'Uncle Will's given me this huge chocolate lolly. Can I eat it now?'

Ally noticed Will looking at her through narrowed eyes and managed a wan smile. 'Yes, sweetheart. Of course you can.'

'Display starting in ten minutes,' Jack said, glancing at his watch and then the crowd gathering around the bonfire.

'Good turnout, Jack.' Molly wrapped her scarf more securely round her throat and smiled at Ally. 'How are you getting on with Sean, dear? I gather he's living with you now.'

'They work very well together,' Will interjected swiftly, taking Ally's arm and guiding her slightly to one side. 'OK, young lady, what's happened?'

Ally gave him a mulish look. This was all his fault. 'I don't know what you mean.'

'Ally…?' Will gave her a gentle smile and she sagged slightly, her eyes bleak as she stared at the blaze of the bonfire.

'We just don't seem to see eye to eye on anything.'

Will raised an eyebrow in disbelief. 'That isn't how it seems from where I'm standing.'

'Then maybe you're standing in the wrong place.' Ally huddled deeper inside her jacket. 'Stop matchmaking, Will. It just causes trouble. I irritate Sean and he drives me totally nuts! Hardly the basis for a harmonious relationship.'

Will gave her a thoughtful look. 'I disagree. Just now, when he was driving you nuts, wasn't he protecting you?'

Ally swallowed and stared across the field at the bonfire surrounded by bobbing figures. 'I suppose so…'

'And when you were walking in the fells on your own—wasn't he protecting you then, too?'

'I don't know.' Ally shrugged and frowned. 'Well, yes, I suppose so, but I don't—'

'You can't blame a man for wanting to protect his woman.'

Oh, for goodness' sake, first her mother and now Will! 'I'm not his woman and I never will be! I'm not the sort of person who can have a quick fling and then wave goodbye while they ride off into the sunset.'

Will gazed at her thoughtfully. 'And you think Sean would do that?'

She gave him an impatient look. 'Of course he would! Sean has never stayed in one place for more than five minutes, has he?'

'That's the legacy of his childhood, I'm afraid. He takes what he can get, never trusts anyone. And, quite frankly, I can't blame him.' Will rubbed his chin slowly and Ally snuggled deeper into her scarf to escape from the biting wind.

'Well, he won't change now.'

Will glanced at her. 'I disagree. What he needs is to fall in love so completely that he has no choice but to change.'

'You've been reading fairy tales, Will.'

For a long moment Ally stared at the crackling bonfire, seeing Sean's face as clearly as if it were in front of her. The arrogant tilt of his jaw, those incredible dark eyes—was there a woman he could fall in love with?

'He's so controlled, Will. I can't see him ever letting go of his emotions.'

Will gave a wry smile. 'Oh, I can. What I can't see is getting him to admit it.'

Ally glanced up and caught the intense look in his eyes. 'Don't look at me, Will. I'm not the right person for Sean.'

Will gave a snort. 'Well, I think you probably are. I can feel the tension between the two of you a mile away.'

Ally shook her head, blushing slightly. 'I admit he probably fancies me, but that's all. Sean wants a compliant woman who'll stay at home and take care of him, not someone who works and goes off walking in the fells on her own. He thinks I'm impulsive and that I take risks. I'm just not his type.'

Will gave a short laugh. 'Oh, don't kid yourself. You're exactly his type.'

Ally swallowed, her voice barely a whisper. 'He'd really hurt me…'

Will gave a small shrug. 'Maybe. Maybe not. Maybe it's worth the risk.'

Worth the risk. That was what Sean had said. But it wasn't a risk she fancied taking. She frowned suddenly. But why not? She took other risks, as Sean was always quick to point out. Why not this one? Casting a glance over her shoulder, her eyes fastened on Sean who was at the farthest end of the field, laughing with one of the mountain rescue team. Even at this distance he looked powerful and male. And very, very attractive.

The sound of her name being shouted made her turn, and she smiled as she saw Jenny Monroe, complete with husband and twins, walking towards her.

'Oh, Dr McGuire, I'm so glad we bumped into you. I just wanted to say thanks for arranging that babysitting for Thursday.'

Ally dragged her blonde hair over one shoulder. 'No problem at all. Were you able to have a good chat with the consultant?'

Jenny exchanged looks with her husband, who nodded. 'He reckons Jen won't need any more surgery because the mole wasn't that deep. He said she'd done well to spot it so early.'

Ally smiled at them both. 'That's really good. I'm so pleased.'

'I need to have regular check-ups.' Jenny bit her lip and shifted one of the twins onto her other hip, 'But he said I shouldn't need any chemotherapy or anything. Can I come and talk to you about it some time? I didn't really understand.'

'Of course. Make an appointment any time that suits you.'

Ally chatted with them for a few more minutes and then they decided the twins were tired and should be in bed so she said goodbye and returned to Will and his group.

Jack was checking that everyone was standing in the right place, ready for the fireworks. Massive bangs and whistles filled the air and the sky lit up to cries of 'Ooh' and 'Ahh'.

Everyone was staring up at the sky when the screams started, loud and terrified, piercing the cold air.

'What the—?' Jack looked round and gasped as he saw a

teenage boy running across the field, flames licking around his body. 'Oh, my God—'

For a split second Ally froze in horror, as did the rest of the spectators, and then she was sprinting towards him.

'Lie down! Stop running,' she yelled, knowing that in his panic he was fanning the flames. He obviously couldn't hear her, and she ran as fast as she could until the breath tore in her throat and pain stabbed her chest. As she drew closer she ripped off her coat, ready to fling it on him, but Sean was there before her.

With a neat rugby tackle he floored the panicking youngster and wrapped him in his jacket, using his hands to beat out the rest of the flames. The boy was still screaming, but the sound was thinner and his eyes were glassy as he stared up at them, his face scorched and blackened.

'Call an ambulance!' Ally snapped at the gathering crowd, and she looked frantically at Sean. 'His clothes are still smouldering. We need to get them off.'

Sean was already removing the charred remains of the boys jacket, and started to gently remove his shirt.

'Get some cold water quickly.' He glanced up at a hovering Red Cross volunteer, who rose to the challenge and sprinted in the direction of the refreshment tent.

'And clingfilm,' Ally called after her, catching Sean's brief nod of approval as together they removed the last piece of charred clothing.

'Good thinking,' he murmured, glancing into the crowd that had gathered. 'We need some gear here. Jack?'

'I'm here.' Jack hurried forward, his face drawn and anxious. 'What do you need?'

'Morphine, oxygen and equipment to intubate,' Ally listed quickly, reaching out to grab the stethoscope Will was proffering. 'Thanks!'

'We need to estimate the surface area and get some fluid into him.' Sean reached out to take the cold water and gently cooled the remaining pieces of charred clothing which could not be removed.

Ally quickly examined the boy, using the rule of nines to calculate how much of the skin was affected. 'Well, it's most of the front, part of the left arm, part of the left leg and part of the back—probably about 28 per cent. Do you agree?'

Sean examined the boy briefly and nodded. 'Looks about right. Mostly full thickness. Let's give him something for the pain quickly.'

Jack handed Ally a box of equipment and she delved into it quickly, removing a large-bore cannula which she deftly inserted into a vein while Sean sorted out the pain relief.

Ally heard the shriek of the ambulance siren and exchanged a look with Sean. 'Thank goodness.'

He nodded. 'Yes. This chap needs hospital help fast. How are his lungs?'

Ally used Will's stethoscope, listening carefully for signs that the smoke or flames had affected his lungs. 'They're clear, actually.'

Sean raked a hand through his hair and let out a breath. 'Thank goodness. OK, let's wrap up these burns and get some fluid into him.'

'How much do you reckon he weighs?' Ally frowned down at the boy, measuring with her eyes. 'Isn't there anyone with him?'

'Doesn't seem to be. The lads are still asking around.' Jack was by her side, waiting for more instructions. 'What do you need?'

'A pen and paper to calculate the fluid replacement…' Sean stood up and rubbed his dark jaw. 'Unless you've got a calculator?'

'We have.' Daniel, the paramedic, sprinted back to the ambulance and returned seconds later. 'It's solar powered so you'll have to stick it under the torch.'

'Thanks.' Sean tapped some figures into the calculator, narrowing his eyes at Ally. 'What do you reckon? Twenty-eight per cent multiplied by his body weight...'

'He must be about 58 kilos,' Ally guessed, and Sean nodded.

'Sounds about right. OK...' He tapped again and calculated the volume of fluid. 'Right—he needs that within four hours so I'll scribble it all down for the hospital.'

Ally jabbed a giving set into the first bag of fluid and attached it to the line in the boy's arm. Then between them they gently wrapped his body in clingfilm to prevent fluid loss and protect the burns, before covering him up to keep him warm.

'Is one of you coming with us?' Daniel pulled the stretcher next to the boy and Sean glanced at Ally with a wry grin.

'My turn, I think. You stay with your daughter.'

She frowned and reached for his right hand which was blackened and sore, turning it over to examine it. 'This doesn't look too healthy. You need to get it seen while you're there.'

In the urgency of the situation she'd forgotten that he'd used his own hands to beat out the last of the flames.

Sean removed his hand from hers and grimaced. 'It hurts like hell so it can't be serious.'

Like him, Ally knew that very serious burns ceased to hurt because of damage to the nerve endings. If Sean could feel his hands then the chances were that the burns were fairly superficial.

'I'd better go. Jack can give you a lift. Will said he'd run my car back when he's finished here, so I'll see you later.' He gave her a brief nod and climbed into the ambulance which drove away as fast as the field and the crowd allowed.

By the time she'd collected Charlie, talked to Will and nabbed a lift home from Jack, it was getting late and she was tired. Fortunately Charlie was, too, and the bedtime routine was completed in record time, leaving her to collapse on one of the huge, squashy sofas which sat on either side of her fireplace. She stared into the flames, thinking first of the boy and his burns and then Mary Thompson. Poor Mary. No wonder she was in a state and worrying about her husband. If the

Thompsons weren't able to come up with a solution themselves, she'd give Mary a ring to discuss possible options.

The wheels of a car crunched on the gravel outside the barn and she sprinted to the door and tugged it open, biting her lip as she saw Sean climb out.

'Are you OK? What happened?'

Sean shrugged and paid the taxi driver, his breath clouding the cold night air. 'They're going to transfer him to the burns unit but he's in a pretty bad way. He's going to be in for a lot of operations, grafting those burns.'

Ally stood back to let him in, frowning slightly as she saw how white and drawn he looked.

'You look really tired. Come in and sit down for a moment.'

He raised an eyebrow, his expression wry. 'I thought I wasn't the flavour of the month.'

'That's just when you behave like a caveman.' Ally gave him a tentative smile, feeling suddenly awkward. 'When you're tired and vulnerable you're OK.'

Sean deposited his length on the sofa and closed his eyes with a groan. 'Well, I'm certainly OK, then. God, I feel awful.'

'They've dressed your hand.'

Sean gave a short laugh and studied the plastic bag over his hand. 'Practical, isn't it? How on earth am I going to see patients with my arm in a bin liner?'

'Don't exaggerate.' Ally put another log on the fire and turned to find him watching her intently. Her heart missed a beat. 'Did they smother it in Flamazine?'

'Definitely.' Sean examined it with wry humour. 'If any bug enters this bag it will be instantly zapped.'

Ally settled herself down in front of the fire, her cheeks pink from the warmth of the flames.

'You won't need it for long and you don't need to do practical things. You can just talk to the patients.'

'Oh, great!' He shrugged himself further into the sofa and stretched out his legs. 'Sorry, Mrs Smith, I can't examine you because I've got a bag on my hand.'

Ally bit her lip. 'You were very brave.'

He raised an eyebrow and laughed. 'Well, if I hadn't done it, you would have so I thought I'd better get there first.'

Despite their earlier row, she had to laugh, too. 'Protecting me again?'

'Isn't that what a man's supposed to do to his woman?'

Her heart stumbled in her chest. 'I'm not your woman.'

'Give me time.' His voice was husky and she shook her head slowly, every nerve in her body tingling.

'You just don't take no for an answer, do you?'

'Never.' His gaze was disconcertingly intense and she blushed awkwardly, picking at a piece of fluff on the rug. Maybe it would help if she changed the subject.

'Can I get you anything? Are you hungry?'

'Very.' His eyes settled on her mouth and then lifted to her face. 'Very hungry.'

Suddenly breathing seemed like hard work. 'You know what I meant...'

'Unfortunately, yes.' He gave a self-deprecating laugh and rose to his feet. 'I don't need food if that's what you're offering. I need my bed. Preferably with you in it.'

A vision of what it would be like to be in bed with him floated through her brain. 'Sean—'

'Come with me.' His voice was husky and he held his good hand, the message in his eyes quite clear.

'I can't.'

He reached down and pulled her to her feet. 'Yes, you can.'

'No.'

He lowered his head, his mouth tantalisingly close to hers. 'Yes...'

The anticipation of his kiss was almost too much, so that when it came she gave a cry of relief and opened her mouth under the pressure of his. This time he kissed her slowly and gently, without the desperate intensity of their previous encounter, but the effect on her highly tuned senses was the same. His tongue seduced hers with a wicked skill until she gave a little cry and struggled to get closer to him. His good arm clamped her against him and she lifted her hands to his hard chest, feeling the strength there before slipping her arms up over the broad shoulders and round his neck.

His muffled curse made her step back, her head swimming and her breathing uneven as she watched him rub his injured hand ruefully. Dear God, what was she doing? How could she say no to a man and then kiss him like that?

'On second thoughts, maybe I will go to bed alone.' Sean brushed her lower lip with his thumb, his smile wry as he glanced at his injured hand. 'When I make love to you I want to have two hands to do it.'

Ally should have been protesting again, denying that it would ever happen, but after the way he'd just made her feel she wasn't capable of saying anything, let alone what she should be saying. So instead she just stood there, her eyes confused, and let him walk away.

The first thing Ally did on Monday morning was to phone Mr Gordon about Jenny Monroe's leg, and was relieved to find him as helpful as she remembered from previous referrals.

'I removed the whole lesion. As you know, the Breslow thickness is still the most useful single indicator of prognosis and Jenny's tumour had only just started to invade the dermis.' The Breslow thickness measured how deeply the tumour had spread into the skin, and it seemed that Jenny's had been removed before it started invading the fatty layer.

Ally tapped her pen on the desk and breathed a sigh of relief. 'So that's good news, then, isn't it?'

'Absolutely.' The consultant sounded as pleased as she felt. 'Obviously I need to follow her up to keep an eye on the scar, and she needs periodic total skin examinations to check for further primary lesions, but basically she should be fine.'

Ally grinned down the phone. 'Thanks, Mr Gordon—I'm so relieved for her.'

He gave a soft laugh. 'Me, too. She's a nice lady.'

Ally replaced the phone and called Jenny immediately, simplifying what the plastic surgeon had said but making it clear that the tumour had been caught very early.

When she was satisfied that Jenny understood the situation and had been reassured, she buzzed through to Helen to let her know she was ready to start her surgery.

'Mr Thompson is here to see you,' Helen's voice came through the intercom. 'Your nine o'clock isn't here yet—can you see him now?'

So he's decided to do something about it, Ally thought, her heart lifting for Mary. 'Yes, send him in.'

Geoff Thompson entered, looking desperately uncomfortable and embarrassed, and more than a little peaky.

'Hello, Mr Thompson.' Ally gave him a quiet smile and gestured for him to sit down.

'I can't believe you can still manage to smile at me after what I did,' he mumbled, rubbing his lined forehead with his large hands.

'You need help, Mr Thompson,' Ally said gently, 'and I assume that's why you're here.'

'Mary and I talked all Sunday. I've never done it before, you know.' His voice was hoarse. 'Never. I've never hit Mary before. Oh, I've been drunk more than I can remember but I've never hit her. I'm just not like that…'

Ally reached forward and touched his hand, anxious to reassure him and build a relationship. 'I believe you, Mr Thompson. Alcohol can make you do all sorts of things that are out of character. We need to talk about what we can do together to solve the problem.'

Geoff Thompson shook his head. 'I've been drinking too much for years, you know. It started socially—I have to drink really as part of my job. You know the score, Dr McGuire—clients, conferences. Before you know it you're drinking regularly every day and the amounts get larger and larger.'

'What do you usually drink?'

He shrugged. 'Wine with meals, spirits in the bar, spirits after a meal.'

Gently Ally probed, delving into his drinking history, finding out when it had started, whether he'd ever tried to cut down or stop, whether he used any other substances.

'I suppose I don't eat properly any more,' he admitted, his expression bleak. 'At least not when I'm working. Mary always has a meal waiting for me at home but, then, she's a wife in a million.'

Ally made a few notes on her pad. 'She's very worried about you.'

'I've let her down so badly.' Suddenly Geoff buried his face in his hands and gave way to tearing sobs. 'I've made such a mess of things. She was so proud of me. So proud.'

'She's still proud,' Ally said firmly, a lump starting in her throat. Poor man. What a mess! 'Just wait one minute, Mr Thompson, while I make a quick call.'

She buzzed through to Helen and quietly asked her to reassign her next three patients to the other partners and bring in some tea.

'Now, listen, we're going to sort this out, Geoff, I promise you that.' She used his first name on purpose, thinking that he needed that extra friendliness. 'But you are going to have to help.'

Geoff rubbed his eyes and took a deep breath, thoroughly embarrassed. 'I'll do anything—I'm so sorry to break down…'

Ally shook her head. 'There's absolutely no need to apologise. Now, this is what we're going to do.' She broke off as Helen entered with the tea, handing Geoff a mug and waiting while he took a few sips. Once Helen had left the room Ally returned to the conversation.

'Now, as far as treatment goes, we have two options. Firstly I could refer you to the Alcohol and Drug Dependence Centre for specialist treatment.'

Geoff pulled a face. 'What's the second option?'

'We could detoxify you at home with the help of the community alcohol team, but that would put a lot of stress on Mary.'

Geoff thought for a minute. 'Mary and I want to overcome this together, which we can do at home. Could we go that route?'

Ally nodded. 'OK. I'll need to do a physical examination and some blood tests.'

Geoff shuddered. 'I hate having blood taken. What's it for?'

'I'm checking your general health, the state of your liver, that sort of thing.' Ally pulled open a drawer and selected several different forms. 'After you've finished here make an appointment with Sister to have your blood taken.'

She scribbled details of the various tests onto the forms and handed them to Geoff, then spent some time exploring his social circumstances, talking about his financial situation, his sex life and his job. She also spent time assessing his mood. Satisfied that he didn't seem clinically depressed, she moved on to this current situation.

'Do you need your car to do your job?'

'Well, I've been lucky.' Geoff gave a wry smile. 'My boss is a pretty good chap and he's found stuff for me to do in the office until I get my licence back.'

'And you can reach the office by train.' Ally nodded and scribbled on the notes again. 'What I'm going to do is to give you a drug called chlordiazepoxide to take over ten days. You'll need time off and very frequent monitoring at first.'

'I can do all that, no problem.'

Ally watched him for a moment, feeling uneasy and not knowing why. Reaching for her phone book, she scribbled down a number and handed it to him. 'That's the number of Alcoholics Anonymous. Do call them because having the support of people in the same situation is invaluable.'

Geoff stared at the number, his jaw set.

'You must realise that you can't drink at all. Controlled drinking just doesn't work when you have a dependence on alcohol.'

'I know that.' Geoff gave a short laugh. 'I'm going to give it my best shot, Dr McGuire. I just hope it works.'

Reaching for the phone, Ally called the community alcohol team and chatted to them, arranging for them to share responsibility for the detoxification programme. Then she sorted out the details with Geoff and watched him go, his shoulders slumped. Would he have the will-power to carry it through?

CHAPTER SEVEN

'I CAN'T believe you were so successful. Good on you!' Will sank into one of the armchairs in the staffroom and smiled at Ally. 'That chap's been drinking for years.'

'Who's been drinking for years?' Sean walked in and glanced at the coffee-pot.

'Can I finish that?'

'Go ahead.' Will stretched his legs out. 'We were talking about Geoff Thompson. Ally detoxed him at home and he's done really well.'

Sean poured himself the last of the coffee and added some milk. 'Did you use the community alcohol team?'

'Oh, yes!' Ally nodded fervently. 'They were marvellous and, frankly, so was his wife. Now we just have to hope he keeps it up. I'm a bit worried about him, really.'

'In what way?' Will tore open a sandwich and started eating his lunch, glancing up as Lucy walked in.

'I don't know exactly.' Ally frowned. 'He doesn't seem clinically depressed but, well, he worries me.'

'Well, it's been a big blow to his ego, that's for sure. It'll take some adjustment, living with what's happened.'

Sean put his coffee on the table and flexed his long fingers. 'I spoke to the burns unit today about Kevin Jones.'

Ally stared at him. 'The boy who was burnt in the fire?'

Sean nodded. 'He's doing better than they hoped, although he's in for a lot of grafting. They think his face should heal perfectly and he should have full use of his hands.'

'Largely thanks to your heroics, I should think. Talking of which…' Will stopped chewing and glanced at Sean quizzically. 'How are yours?'

'Fully recovered, thanks.' Sean gave him a brief smile and

held out his hands for inspection. 'Jack found out the story, by the way. Apparently, he was mucking around with some friends on the waste ground behind the field, and one of them put a firework in his pocket.'

'Oh, no!' Ally clapped her hand over her mouth.

Sean gave a grim smile. 'Oh, yes. Of course, when the thing went off they panicked and legged it, leaving him to sort himself out. It was lucky for him we were all so near.'

'Poor, poor thing!' Ally shook her head, horrified. 'Still, it must have reassured Jack a bit. He was fretting that it was something to do with the mountain rescue function.'

'Well, they made a fortune apparently, despite the drama.' Will screwed up the empty sandwich packet and tossed it into the bin. 'Good thing, too. They need some new equipment. Anyway, what are you two up to this weekend, seeing as you're both off?'

Ally rummaged in the fridge for her cheese roll, wishing Will would be more subtle. 'I'm going walking. Mum's having Charlie for the weekend to help fill the freezer for Christmas, so I'm off.' She rocked back on her heels, her expression fierce as her eyes challenged Sean's. 'And don't you dare lecture me!'

'Would I?' His dry tone made her smile and she sat back down in her chair and nibbled her roll.

'I promise to leave my intended route with Jack.'

Sean was looking at her thoughtfully. 'I don't suppose you want company?'

The roll suddenly jammed in her throat. 'Company?'

He gave a lopsided grin. 'Well, if I promise not to make one single chauvinistic comment, can I join you?'

The sudden rush of pleasure she felt astonished and horrified her. She should be keeping her distance, not seeking his company. The answer had to be no.

'Yes.' His eyes held hers for a long moment and she read the surprise and the question in them. He was wondering why she'd said yes. The trouble was, so was she. Why on earth had she said yes when she meant no? 'But be warned—the first big-brother comment you make, I push you over the edge.'

Sean laughed and raised his hands in a gesture of submission, his eyes gleaming. 'I love a dominant woman!'

Will glanced at them curiously and then suddenly concentrated very hard on his sandwich. 'You'd better take him, Ally, otherwise he'll be staring at the fells waiting for you to come down, calling Jack and the team every ten minutes.'

Lucy beamed at them. 'You can call me, too, if you like because Red and I passed our assessment last night.'

'Oh, Lucy, that's great!' Ally leaped up and gave her a hug. 'So she's now an official search dog?'

'She certainly is.' Lucy peeled a banana and curled her slim legs under her bottom, a pleased expression on her pretty face.

Sean frowned. 'Who calls you out if there's an incident, then? Jack?'

Lucy nodded. 'Either him or Howard Davies, the SARDA co-ordinator.'

SARDA, the Search And Rescue Dog Association—Ally knew how many lives they'd saved over the years.

She grinned. 'So now you have your own pager?'

'I do, indeed.' Lucy cocked her head on one side and gave a flippant grin. 'So I can dump my patients on you lot and dash off to the rescue.'

'Well, I don't want you rescuing us, thanks!' Ally finished her apple and tossed the core into the bin.

'Where are you planning to go?' Sean stretched his long legs out and Ally tried not to notice how the fabric showed the hard muscle of his thighs. Since the bonfire party they'd hardly seen each other, mostly due to conflicting on-call demands, and she was horrified by how much the fact bothered her. Also, if she was honest, she was more than a little disappointed that he hadn't really gone out of his way to seek her out. Maybe he'd changed his mind about her—maybe. She gave herself a sharp talking to. So what if he'd changed his mind? That was good, wasn't it? That was exactly what she wanted.

Realising that Sean was waiting for an answer, Ally shook herself. 'Um…depends on the weather.'

She removed a crumb from her lip with the tip of her tongue, colour seeping into her cheeks as she caught Sean's eyes on her mouth. For a brief second their eyes held and her heart lurched as she read the message in his. He hadn't changed his mind. He was biding his time. The knowledge made her nerve endings tingle.

'You were saying?' His eyes teased her and she looked away, flustered.

'I don't know—maybe the Fairfield Horseshoe.'

Will frowned and glanced out of the window. 'Well, for goodness' sake, check the weather and be careful, the pair of you.'

'Yes, Uncle Will.' Sean grinned and it occurred to Ally that he hadn't said anything else about leaving. Had he changed his mind about that and decided to stay on in the practice for a while? She gave herself another sharp talking to. So what if he had? It wasn't any of her business. It wouldn't change the way he felt about relationships—or the way she felt about men who didn't want commitment.

Her afternoon antenatal clinic was busy and her nerves were jangling by the time Felicity Webster walked in, two children strapped securely in their buggy.

'I know you're not supposed to bring buggies through to the consulting rooms, but Helen said it would be fine and I—'

'Felicity,' Ally interrupted gently, 'it's no problem. It's a rule that's meant to be broken in cases such as yours. I wouldn't fancy trying to examine you with those two on the loose.'

Felicity dropped into a chair, clearly exhausted. 'Well, I certainly can't carry them.'

'How's the chickenpox?'

'Oh, it's cleared up nicely.' She leaned forward and tugged

a woolly hat off one of the children. 'Tom's still got scabs, but we're managing to stop him scratching.'

Ally had a brief look. 'Oh, that's looking fine. And what about you?'

Felicity gave a short laugh. 'What about me? I'm due tomorrow, and if it doesn't come soon I'm sending it back.'

Ally grinned. 'Any twinges?'

'Plenty.' Felicity shifted slightly, obviously uncomfortable. 'But none that have made this baby pop out.'

'When's your next hospital appointment?'

'Next week.' Felicity pulled a face. 'But it's got to come before then. I'm stuffing myself with raspberry tea, pineapples—you name it, I'm doing it.'

'Well, let's have a look at you.' Ally checked Felicity's blood pressure, examined her ankles and fingers for signs of swelling and tested her urine. 'That's all fine, Felicity. Hop up on the couch and I'll take a look at the baby.'

'Hop?' Felicity grinned and eased herself up, hobbling painfully over to the couch. 'I could be wrong but I don't think I'll ever hop again.'

Ally laughed. 'You will. With two under five and a new baby you'll spend all day hopping.'

'Don't! I can't even bear to think about how I'm going to manage.' Felicity wriggled down and exposed her bump. 'It feels huge.'

Ally slid her hands over Felicity's abdomen, palpating the lie of the baby. 'Not at all. I think it's a nice size.'

'That's because you're not the one who has to have it,' Felicity said dryly.

'True.' Ally laughed and picked up the Sonicaid. 'The baby's in a good position. Let's have a listen.'

The rhythmic galloping of the foetal heartbeat echoed around the room and they exchanged smiles.

'Oh, lovely!' Felicity grinned and then sobered. 'I'm dreading it, Dr McGuire. I know you keep telling me not to panic but I keep thinking of the other two…'

'I know you'll be fine this time.' Ally switched off the Sonicaid. 'What are you doing with the other two when you go in with this one?'

'Oh, my mum will come. She's only ten minutes away.'

Ally helped her to sit up and scribbled on her notes while Felicity straightened her clothing.

'Well, I don't think this baby will be here for a few days yet.'

'Really?' Felicity chewed her lip. 'I don't know whether to be pleased or sorry. Sometimes you wonder whether they're more trouble out than in.'

Ally laughed as she opened the door and helped her with the buggy. 'Make sure you let me know if anything happens.'

Felicity grinned. 'You'll probably hear the yelling. Thanks, Dr McGuire.'

Ally tucked the map back into her pocket and lifted her face to the wind.

'Fantastic, isn't it?' Sean stared at the view, his hard features relaxed and contented.

'Yes. I love this time of year.' Ally's cheeks were pink from the cold and strands of blonde hair had escaped from her woolly hat, framing her face. 'No tourists.'

Sean glanced up at the sky and frowned slightly. 'I don't like the look of that.'

Ally followed his gaze and shrugged. 'The forecast was good.'

'Yes.' Sean didn't seem convinced, staring at the sky with narrowed eyes.

'Did you do a lot of outdoor stuff in the army?'

He turned to look at her with a smile that melted her bones. 'Oh, yes. We used to have to spend days at a time outside under the stars. Survival training.'

'You lucky thing—being paid to spend days in the mountains.'

He gave a short laugh. 'Well, it wasn't always a bed of roses.

The Brecon Beacons covered in snow in the middle of winter isn't the most inviting terrain.'

Ally carried on up the path, falling into step behind him. 'It must have been dangerous.'

'Oh, it was.' Sean hitched his rucksack more comfortably on his back. 'The army loses people on exercise far more often than they like to admit.'

'When did you decide you wanted to be a doctor?'

He stopped walking and leaned against a rock, staring across the stark mountain scenery.

'I don't know, really. I suppose subconsciously I must have thought about it when I lived with Will and Molly. But I didn't really get interested until I did some medic training in the army.'

'How did you come to live with Will?' Ally blushed as he turned to look at her. 'Sorry. Forget I asked. I know you hate talking about it.'

He gave a short laugh. 'I'm surprised the gossips haven't given you the story already.'

Ally's voice was quiet. 'I'm not a gossip, Sean.'

His eyes held hers. 'I know you're not.'

Her heart thudded under the intensity of his gaze. Was he going to kiss her? He hadn't kissed her for ages. Not since the night of the bonfire party. She was horrified by how much she wanted him to. What was the matter with her?

'I was a bit of a handful when I was young.' He stared at the horizon and gave a wry smile. 'Actually, that's an understatement. I was the boy from hell. I suppose it's not surprising that I was moved from one foster-home to another. No one could put up with me for long. I was totally wild.'

Ally's heart contracted, thinking of how lonely and desperate it must have been for him with no family of his own. No wonder he'd been a handful. It was amazing that he'd grown up to be so well balanced. Part of her longed to ask if he'd ever tried to contact his mother, but he was opening up more than he ever had before and she didn't want to jeopardise that with intrusive questions.

'So where did Will come into it?' Suddenly she wanted to put her arms round him and hold him tight. To love him like he'd never been loved before.

Love him?

Her breath caught. Dear God, she was a total fool but she did love him. As well as the strong, tough man, she'd had glimpses of the scared boy, protecting his emotions, and she loved him, too.

'Well, he and Molly—' Sean broke off suddenly and frowned down at her. 'Are you all right?'

No. She wasn't. She was in love with a man who never wanted commitment. The realisation made her feel strange.

'I'm fine.'

'Right…' Sean stared at her for a moment and then carried on. 'He and Molly had fostered once before but they didn't do it regularly. Then one day I got into trouble and Will bailed me out.'

Ally gave him a curious look. 'What did he do?'

Sean stared at the mountains and gave a short laugh. 'I'd broken into a warehouse, only I misjudged the drop between the window and the floor and I hurt myself. My friends took me to the surgery and Will was the duty doctor.'

'And he sorted you out?'

'He stitched my leg, jabbed me and then gave me the sternest talking to I'd ever had. We talked for hours.' Sean kicked some loose stones on the path and gave a wry smile. 'I kept waiting for him to call the police but he never did. He called Social Services and read them the Riot Act.'

'For not keeping a proper eye on you, and placing you with the wrong families?'

'Something like that. Anyway, the long and the short of it was that he and Molly took me in. And that was that.'

'Only you'd spent too long running wild, with no one bothering about you, to be able to trust them.'

Sean turned to look at her. 'What makes you so astute?'

She swallowed. 'I don't know. It's just the obvious reaction, I suppose.' And he was still running, she knew that much.

'Well, I did learn to trust them eventually but it was Will who steered me towards the army. I always loved fitness and the outdoor life and I suppose he thought the discipline and training would do me good. He was right.'

'But he must have been thrilled when you decided to be a doctor.'

Sean's eyes softened. 'He was.'

'He loves you.'

'I know that.' Sean's voice was gruff and he straightened and shifted his rucksack more comfortably on his shoulders. 'And what about you? Your childhood was idyllic by comparison, wasn't it?'

They stomped up the path, continuing to talk, and Ally gasped with shock when Sean suddenly stopped and she cannoned into him.

'Sorry—you need brake lights! What's the matter?'

'The weather. Damn. I should have trusted my instincts.' Sean stared at the blackening sky and braced himself against the wind.

Ally blinked with shock. She hadn't even noticed the weather. All she'd been thinking of had been Sean, Sean, and Sean. But as she stopped walking the wind suddenly buffeted her, making her stumble into him. 'We'd better get down fast.'

Sean hesitated and then gave a brief nod. 'Yes, OK. We'll give it a try.'

Give it a try? What did he mean by that?

Walking as close to him as she could, she dipped her head to give herself some protection from the wind, her eyes narrowing against the sharp raindrops which started to pelt against her face.

'Don't you just love Lake District weather?' Sean's voice was barely audible above the wind as they exchanged a wry look of understanding.

They struggled on for another half-hour, Ally forcing her tired limbs forward despite the force of the wind which pushed her back again.

When Sean finally stopped walking she fought to stay upright against the pressure of the howling wind, and only Sean's firm grip on her hand stopped her from dropping to the ground with exhaustion. Why on earth hadn't they noticed the change in the weather and how late it was? She bit her lip. Because they'd been too busy enjoying each other's company, that was why. Neither of them had paid too much attention to the weather.

The wind threw all its force at her again and she stumbled against Sean who clamped her against him with a strong arm. For once she was glad of his protection.

He steadied them both and frowned down into her white face. 'Are you OK?'

She nodded, not wanting to show how scared she was. She knew better than anyone how totally unforgiving these mountains were when you made a mistake. And they'd made a mistake. A big one. And it was winter.

Sean's eyes swept her strained features and then he glanced at his watch. 'It's getting late. We'd better set up camp.'

'Camp?'

Her gloved hand fastened itself to the front of his jacket. He represented the only solid security around here and she wasn't letting go, principles or no principles!

Sean grimaced and his fingers closed reassuringly over hers. 'We're not going to make it down before dark. I'm sorry. I misjudged it really badly.'

'It wasn't your fault.' She was almost shouting to be heard above the noise of the wind. 'You weren't responsible for me.'

He gave a wry smile and flicked the end of her chilled nose with his gloved finger. 'Miss Independent.'

She managed to return the smile—just. 'Can't we just push on and make it down? We've got torches...'

Sean shook his head. 'No way. The wind's rising. We've

loused up badly, sweetheart, so we either make the team drag themselves out to rescue us or we camp and sit it out until morning.'

Ally stared at him. 'We haven't got the equipment.'

Sean gave her a saucy grin. 'You keep refusing to let me show you my equipment.'

How could he flirt and be so relaxed when they were in danger? 'Sean, please…'

Something in her voice must have penetrated because his smile faded and his eyes were gentle. 'We'll be fine, angel. Trust me.' Gently disentangling her hand from his jacket, he checked the map and the compass. 'OK, let's set up the tent on the lee slope. Can you walk just a bit farther?'

She nodded dumbly, staring at him in amazement. Tent? He had a tent? They walked on for another ten minutes and then he stopped abruptly and swung the rucksack off his massive shoulders. In a remarkably short time—and with no help from her—he'd set up a dome tent.

'Right. All wet clothes off quickly and into that polythene bag, and then get inside fast.' Sean helped drag off her dripping wet jacket and over-trousers and left her to undo her boots while he sorted himself out. She stuffed her wet clothes into the polythene bag so that they wouldn't get the inside of the tent wet, and crawled inside.

Seconds later he joined her, his dark hair glistening with a mixture of rain and snow.

'OK?' He paused as he tugged some more gear out of his rucksack, a frown touching his dark features. 'You're shivering.'

'I'm fine.' She *was* shivering but goodness knew why. The tent was totally waterproof and windproof and was the perfect shelter.

'Strip some more clothes off and get into the sleeping bag.' Sean gave the bag a vigorous shake and threw a sleeping mat in her direction. 'Spread that under the bag.'

She followed his orders without question, too cold and exhausted to argue, watching while he secured the tent and fished in his rucksack for the mobile phone.

'You're calling Jack?'

'We gave him our route so he'll be worrying soon. Let's hope there's a signal.' Sean punched in the number and then grinned. 'Jack? It's us.' He listened for a moment and then gave a grim laugh. 'Tell me about it!'

Ally could hear Jack's voice, but not what he was saying.

Sean's eyes rested on her face. 'No, she's fine. Just a bit tired out.' He listened again and this time his jaw tightened. 'No need, but thanks for the offer. We'll camp out here tonight and then I'll get her down at first light.'

Jack must have said something else because Sean gave a short laugh and muttered, 'In my dreams.' Then he snapped the phone shut and dropped it back into the rucksack.

'Right, then.' He stripped off his jumper and thick shirt and raised an eyebrow in her direction. 'I suppose you're going to say I can't share the sleeping bag.'

How could she possibly say that when it was his skill and preparation that was saving them both? She shook her head numbly and shuffled to the furthest edge to make room for him. Even so, it was a shock to her system when he slid inside with her, the warmth and power of his body filling the remaining space in the sleeping bag. Outside the wind screamed in anger and whipped at the sides of the tent, and Ally snuggled further inside the sleeping bag, a delicious feeling of safety creeping over her as she felt Sean next to her.

'I ought to turn the torch off.' Sean's voice was gruff and she shifted her head so that she could look at him.

'Can we keep it on a bit longer?'

He lifted a hand and brushed a strand of blonde hair away from her face as he searched her eyes with a frown. 'Are you scared?'

She shook her head. 'No.' It was true. She wasn't. But only because he was here and she felt totally safe with him. 'I just don't want it to be dark yet.'

He studied her for a long moment and then rolled onto his back, staring at the roof of the tent.

Ally gazed at his strong profile, hardly daring to breathe. Why didn't he touch her? After all their previous encounters she would have thought that the first thing he'd do in this situation when they were both half-naked would be to carry on his seduction. But he didn't. He didn't touch her, and she found herself almost moaning aloud in frustration. This was ridiculous. Usually she was fighting him off and now, when she desperately wanted him to touch her, he seemed totally indifferent to her. She wanted him to touch her so badly. She needed to feel his strength, needed his comfort. She loved him so much—so much. Sean was right. It *was* worth the risk.

She was still lying on her side and unconsciously her left hand crept onto his chest, her fingertips feeling the hard muscle beneath the fabric of his T-shirt. Without even planning to do so, she slipped her fingers underneath, her stomach flipping as they tangled with the hair on his chest.

Sean sucked in his breath and shackled her hand. 'You're playing with fire.'

She lifted herself on one elbow, her breath catching in her throat as she met his burning gaze.

'Sean?' Her voice was a plea, and he closed his eyes briefly, the muscles in his throat working as he swallowed.

'Let's get one thing straight, shall we?' His voice was husky. 'I may have amazing will-power when we're both fully clothed and cavorting around the health centre, but you're half-naked in my sleeping bag, angel, and if you carry on like this I can't promise not to retaliate.'

Ally moved so that her body was pressed against his and slipped one slim, smooth calf over his hair-roughened thigh so that she was half lying on top of him.

'I think I want you to retaliate.' Her words were so soft that she barely heard them herself, and for a moment she wondered whether she'd said them at all. Maybe she'd just thought them.

Then Sean stabbed his fingers through her long blonde hair

and anchored the back of her head so that she couldn't look away.

A muscle flickered in his jaw and his gaze was intent. 'Say that again.'

She swallowed hard. 'I want you Sean…'

He stared at her for a long moment and shook his head slowly, his expression grim. 'No. No, you don't. It's just because you're scared and you think you need me. You don't need to worry, Ally. I promise to get you off this mountain safely.'

'It's not that.'

His eyes held hers, his strong fingers clamped either side of her head.

'What, then?'

'You were right.' Her heart was hammering in her chest. She'd never propositioned a man in her life. What if he turned her down? Didn't want her any more?

'Right about what?'

'About it being worth the risk.' Her voice was a whisper, and when he didn't react she lowered her head slightly and licked at his lips in a provocative gesture that made him catch his breath.

In one swift movement Sean rolled her on her back, using enough of his ample strength to keep her pinned under him but not enough to hurt her.

The muscles in one shoulder bunched as he supported most of his weight and his free hand came up and cupped her chin, forcing her to look directly at him. Not that she wanted to look anywhere else. She was through with playing games. She loved this man with all her heart and she no longer cared about what was sensible. She'd deal with the consequences later. All she cared about was now…

'This is your final warning.' The look in his dark eyes made her limbs weaken, and she curled a hand behind his strong neck.

'Kiss me, Sean.'

He lowered his head, his breathing uneven, his eyes still holding hers, still checking for her reaction as his mouth closed over hers. And then he gave a groan and was lost. And so was she. The storm outside the tent faded into insignificance compared to the one raging inside.

His kiss was wild and dominating, and his body shifted over hers, his arousal immediately obvious as she felt him press closer to her. Her insides were melting with the heat of sensation, and she sobbed his name as his hand jerked her T-shirt up and found the catch of her bra.

The touch of his fingers on her breast made her writhe in an agony of yearning and she curled a leg around him to try and bring him closer.

'Steady angel.' He lifted his head, his breathing ragged as he stared at her, his hand moving downwards.

'Sean, please…'

'Not yet…' He slid down further inside the sleeping bag and she gasped as she felt the warmth of his tongue touch her sensitised breasts. Heat flooded her cheeks as his hand slid further down still and found what he was searching for, his fingers stroking her with wicked intimacy.

'Please…' She was writhing under his skilled touch and he lifted his head, his eyes glittering as they focused on her glazed eyes.

'I've wanted you for so long…'

'I want you, too…' She was going to die. If he didn't make love to her soon she was definitely going to die.

He paused for a moment, his jaw tense. 'Are you protected?'

She hesitated briefly and then nodded. It would be all right. It was totally the wrong time of the month and she wanted this man. Oh, she wanted him so badly.

This time when he held her she felt the power of his arousal, felt him part her legs and take her mouth again in a kiss that reflected the wild hunger between them.

He entered her with a powerful thrust, and she thought her sudden cry of pain had been lost in his mouth as the heat and the agony mingled inside her. But he must have felt her sudden tension because he froze and lifted his head.

'Ally?' He stared at her in utter confusion and she shook her head, sliding her hands over his hard buttocks to stop him withdrawing.

'No! Don't stop…'

'Stop? You think I'm Superman?' He gave a soft groan and kissed the tip of her nose, obviously fighting his hunger for her. 'I don't think I could stop if you begged me but that doesn't mean I want to hurt you.'

'You're not hurting me now. It was just for a second.' She gasped and stroked a hand over his satiny flesh. 'Please, Sean…'

His breathing was laboured. 'Why the hell didn't you say something?'

'It's not relevant.'

He moved slightly and frowned as her nails curled into his skin. 'Relax, sweetheart. It won't hurt if you relax. Trust me angel.'

So she did. And once she relaxed the pain went, and Sean stayed very still, kissing her gently, nibbling and licking at her lips until she was desperate for more. With a mew of impatience she shifted under him and he gave a sharp intake of breath and captured her face in his hand, forcing her to look at him. And then she felt him move inside her, powerful and male yet still touchingly careful with her. He held her gaze, watching her intently, and then with a grunt he dropped his head onto her shoulder and scooped up her hips so that they were joined even more closely.

'Oh, Sean!' The closeness was like nothing she'd ever felt before, but like everything she'd ever dreamed of in all her secret fantasies. The feelings overwhelmed her and instinctively she wrapped her legs around him, his harsh breathing confirming just how much control it was taking for him to hold back.

But she didn't want him to hold back. Not any more. The

pain had gone, and with it any shyness and inhibition she might have had. She wanted it all, everything he could give, and she was ready to give back in full measure. She stroked her hand teasingly up his back and moved her hips under his, feeling a thrill of excitement as she felt him respond.

'You're a witch.' He kissed her again, his tongue delving deeply inside her, and she moved restlessly under him.

'Sean, please...' Her sob of need was trapped by his searching mouth and he growled deep in his throat and thrust deeply inside her.

'Better?'

'Oh, yes!' She arched towards him, their bodies moving as one until the pressure burst and her cries of fulfilment mingled with his harsh groan as he shuddered against her.

Tears seeped from under her closed lids and she heard him give a muffled curse, before wrapping her in his arms and rolling them both so that she lay almost on top of him.

'I'm sorry, sweetheart.' His voice was a groan of apology. 'I was too rough.'

'No.' Her voice was little more than a whisper and he stroked the blonde hair away from her damp cheek and ran a thumb over her bottom lip. 'You weren't rough.'

His grip on her tightened. 'I made you cry, for heaven's sake.'

She turned her head and gave him a watery smile. 'Because you made it so fantastic, and I never guessed it would ever feel like that.'

He stared at her for a long moment and then closed his eyes briefly. 'There's so much you need to tell me but somehow I just don't want to hear it yet.'

That was fine by her. She snuggled closer into the warmth of his body, her smooth skin sliding over his rougher, muscled thighs.

'Carry on like that and we won't get any sleep tonight,' Sean warned, his mouth tantalisingly close to hers.

Her heart raced. 'Who needs sleep?'

He stared at her and his mouth curved into the sexiest smile she'd ever seen. 'Who, indeed...'

CHAPTER EIGHT

THEY were up at first light, packing up the tent and the rest of the gear and struggling into their walking clothes.

Sean didn't say much as they walked down the mountain and, staring at his massive shoulders leading the way down the narrow path, Ally felt a twinge of disquiet. Something was wrong. After the intimacy they'd shared during the night he should have been holding her hand or casting her the odd tender smile. Instead, his hard features were set and grim, his whole attitude one of single-minded intent as he concentrated on getting them down the mountain.

Part of her longed to put her arms round him and tell him how much she loved him, but pride stopped her. This was Sean, after all, and she knew he kept his emotions firmly in check. Except for last night. Her body warmed as she remembered the details of the night before. How he'd held her, touched her, driven them both to incredible heights of sensation and emotion. But he'd never mentioned love.

Had the emotion been all hers and not his? Had she imagined the soft way he'd spoken and touched her? Maybe that was all part of his seduction technique. Oh, heck, what was the matter with her? She lifted her chin and walked a little more briskly. She'd known all along that Sean didn't want emotional involvement—he'd made it clear enough, hadn't he? So what had she expected? That he'd drop on one knee and declare undying love?

Yes, she admitted miserably, suddenly stopping dead and staring at the path in front of her. That was exactly what she'd expected, or at least hoped for. But it had just been a fantasy. It wasn't going to be like that. Sean's rule was no commitment and she'd thought she could play by that rule, but she'd been wrong. She couldn't have a short-lived affair with this man. One night had been bad enough. The memories left her breathless, desperate for more, and she knew that time would just make it worse for her.

She just wasn't the sort of person who could have a fling, have fun while it lasted and then move on to someone else. She was a constant person, someone who believed that when you loved someone it was for ever. And she loved Sean.

'Are you all right?'

She blinked, suddenly aware that Sean had stopped and was frowning down at her.

'I'm fine.'

'Are you hurt or something?'

Part of her wanted to scream at him. Of course she was hurt! How could he possibly not understand that? She was in agony. It depressed her to admit just how self-contained and controlled he was this morning. Didn't he care at all, for goodness' sake? Obviously not. Well, push on, Ally, she told herself grimly. Just get home and then you can work out what you're going to do.

She summoned up a casual smile that cost her more in effort than the entire walk had. 'I'm fine. Just admiring the view.'

For a brief second she thought she saw a shadow flit across his face and then it was gone.

'Good. Let's crack on, then.'

She followed him on autopilot, her legs feeling like lead as she picked her way over the rocks towards the bottom of the valley.

They met Jack, coming up. His eyes gleamed when he saw them.

'Just checking up on you.'

Sean gave him a wry look. 'Go on, say it. What the hell were we playing at?'

Jack laughed and rested a foot on a rock, surveying the view with obvious pleasure. 'Enjoying yourselves, I imagine.'

Ally blushed furiously. 'Sorry, Jack.'

'What for?' Jack shrugged and fell into step beside her. 'You didn't drag me out of my bed.'

'We must have worried you.'

Jack glanced across at Sean. 'Can't say you did, really. If I had to get lost on a mountain with someone and it couldn't be Jennifer Aniston, I suppose I'd be glad it was Sean.'

Ally stared at Sean, her eyes skimming over his powerful physique, remembering the way he'd made love to her—despite everything, she was glad it had been Sean, too...

'Can I give you a lift home?' Jack gestured towards his van in the car park, but Sean shook his head and caught Ally's arm in a vice-like grip.

'No, thanks. We need to sort out this gear and have a debrief.'

'A debrief?' Ally glanced over her shoulder and waved as Jack pulled away, before turning back to Sean who was unlocking his car.

He gave a wry smile and heaved their gear into the boot. 'I think we've got things to talk about, don't you?'

Somehow that didn't sound very lover-like and Ally's mouth dried. If he was regretting last night then she certainly didn't want him to spell it out. She was much too tired for a confrontation.

They both climbed into the car and Sean started the engine, his breath clouding the freezing air until the interior of the car slowly warmed up.

Finally he turned towards her, a muscle working in his cheek. 'Right, then. Confession time.'

'Confession?' Ally blinked, confused. This wasn't what she'd expected. 'What do you mean, confession?'

He frowned impatiently. 'Oh, come on, Ally! Don't play more games. How come I found myself making love to a virgin instead of a woman with a child of five?'

Her heart was thundering in her chest. He seemed angry. Why would that make him angry? 'Why does it matter?'

'Because you lied to me, dammit!' He slammed the palm of

his hand against the steering-wheel and drew a deep breath, obviously controlling his temper with difficulty. 'OK. Let's start at the beginning. Who the hell is Charlie's real mother, then?'

'My sister.'

There was a long silence and then he turned to look at her, his expression baffled.

'Your sister?' He shook his head slightly as if to clear it. Obviously he was also suffering from the total lack of sleep. 'The one who died?'

Ally nodded. 'She was madly in love with Rob, even though she knew he didn't care that much about her.'

'Hold on, let me get this straight.' He rubbed his temples with those long, strong fingers and took a deep breath. 'Rob was her boyfriend, not yours?'

'That's right.'

'And she got pregnant?'

'It was an accident.' Ally stared out of the window, not seeing the outline of the fells that she loved so much. All she could see was her sister's face. 'She rang me and told me and she was so thrilled—you can't imagine.'

Sean's voice was rough. 'Even knowing that Rob was a louse?'

'Even knowing that.' Ally's tone was soft and wistful and she glanced down at her fingers, surprised to find them tangling in her jacket. 'Needless to say, Rob didn't hang around.'

'But she carried on with the pregnancy?' He sounded surprised and Ally rounded on him, her eyes challenging.

'Of course she carried on with it!' Her blue eyes blazed. 'We're like that in our family, you see. We love babies and children. We believe totally in marriage and commitment, and if something does go wrong we all stick together. No way would Fay have had a termination. She knew we'd all rally round and help out.'

'So what happened?' The hard edge had gone from his voice and Ally closed her eyes and shook her head.

'The crazy thing is, I don't even really know—it was so quick. One day we were shopping together for baby things and she was telling me how well she was and how excited, the next we had a call from the consultant at the hospital, whom I knew vaguely, telling me that she'd been admitted and was in a critical state.'

Sean frowned. 'With what?'

'Pre-eclampsia.' Ally stared at her fingernails. 'Seems daft, doesn't it? People still dying of pre-eclampsia in this day and age, but that was what happened. Her blood pressure shot up, her liver enzymes were all over the place, she went into massive liver failure and died. It was so quick.'

Sean hesitated. 'I'm sorry.'

Ally shrugged and blinked away the tears. 'Yes, well, they delivered the baby, obviously, hoping that it would improve her condition, but it made no difference.'

'So you were left with a tiny baby with no mother or father.'

Ally's jaw clenched. 'Not exactly. Rob appeared on the scene once he found out what had happened.'

'He wanted the baby?' Sean sounded surprised and Ally's laugh was bitter.

'No.' Her fingers curled into her jacket as she fought to control her anger. 'He wanted money. And plenty of it.'

'Money?' Sean's eyes narrowed. 'What for?'

'For letting us keep the baby.'

There was a long silence and then the breath hissed through his teeth. 'Let me get this straight. The guy wanted you to pay him for leaving you alone—is that right?'

'In a nutshell.'

Sean gave her an odd look. 'And knowing you, I'll bet you gave it to him.'

She held his gaze defiantly. 'Of course I did. What choice did I have? She was Fay's baby. I couldn't let him take her. He was threatening to have her adopted.'

For a moment he was silent, his expression unreadable. 'So what did you do?'

'What do you think?' Ally turned her head away from his and stared back out of the window. 'I paid him every penny he asked for.'

Sean shook his head slowly, disbelief written all over his features. 'And your parents agreed?'

'They didn't know.' Ally's expression was blank. 'They still don't. They were so devastated by Fay's death, the last thing they needed was to battle for Charlie as well. I used all the savings I had and—well, Will helped me. I just wanted that rat away from my family.'

There was a long silence. 'So you gave him all your money and borrowed more?'

Ally nodded. 'You probably think I'm stupid, but I couldn't see any other way out at the time.'

'And that's why you still struggle financially?'

'Yes.' Ally gave a small smile. 'It's getting easier. I've paid Will back. I just don't have much to throw around.'

'You did all that for a little girl who wasn't even yours?' Sean was looking at her strangely. 'And that's why you left the mountain rescue team?'

'Of course.' She turned to him, her blue eyes huge in her pale face. 'My whole life changed. What choice did I have?'

He stared at her for a long moment and then seemed to shake himself. 'Why didn't you tell me this before?'

'Because it isn't something we broadcast,' Ally said simply. 'Charlie knows. She's always known who her real mother is, but we just don't talk about it unless we have to.' It was too painful.

For a long moment Sean was silent and then he let his breath out in a hiss. 'OK. That explains a lot, but not why you were still a virgin at twenty-eight.'

She blushed hotly and looked away. 'That's my business.'

'Maybe it was until last night.' He tucked a finger under her chin and drew her face round to look at him, his eyes searching. 'Now it's very much my business, too. You're a beautiful woman, Ally. Why didn't some man lock you away with him years ago?'

She gave an embarrassed laugh, trying to suppress the rush of pleasure she felt that he still thought she was beautiful.

'Blame it on the fairy tale.'

He frowned. 'The fairy tale?'

'You know…' She gave a shrug which was more casual than her feelings. 'Boy meets girl, one true love, happy ever after—that sort of thing.'

He nodded slowly. 'Right. And that's what you believed in?'

'Until Charlie came along…'

'But she was Fay's.'

'Yes, but I saw what a rat Rob was and…' She stared down at her hands and gave a wry smile. 'And I was actually going out with someone when it all happened.'

'Don't tell me.' Sean's voice was harsh. 'He vanished into the sunset as well.'

Ally nodded and gave a light-hearted shrug that hid the pain. 'In a trail of dust. His exact words were "No way do I want to be saddled with a screaming baby who isn't even mine."'

'So you gave up on your dream.'

'Well, I was certainly disillusioned.' The trouble was, she hadn't given up on the dream. Not entirely. Which was why she'd always avoided the countless matchmaking attempts that had come her way. She'd always been convinced that somewhere out there Mr Right existed. And then she'd met Sean. She glanced sideways at him and their eyes locked.

Her heart missed a beat as she remembered everything that had happened between them, how it had felt. Her voice was barely a whisper. 'You regret it, don't you?'

Even if the answer caused her pain, she needed to know. She just wasn't the sort of person who played games. She liked things to be honest and straightforward.

He hesitated just a moment too long. 'No…'

Disappointment slammed through her body. 'Obviously it didn't live up to expectation.'

He used a word that shocked her, his eyes suddenly angry. 'You know that isn't true.'

'Do I?' Her gaze met his, her eyes clear and honest, his wary and uncomfortable. 'Then what's the problem, Sean? And don't tell me there's no problem because ever since we woke up this morning you've treated me as if I was a major embarrassment.'

'Dammit, Ally, you know what the problem is!' he muttered under his breath, and closed his eyes briefly. 'You'd never slept with a man before, for goodness' sake. It was hardly casual for you, was it?'

'Oh, I see now.' She gave a short laugh and stared out of the window to hide her pain. 'We're back to that dreaded word "commitment". Ally hasn't slept with a man before, so if she slept with you it must mean she's already booked the church.'

'Ally—'

'No. Don't say any more.' She clicked her seat belt in place with shaking hands and stared straight ahead. 'I'm tired and I need a shower. Just take me home, please, Sean.'

He didn't move. 'We haven't finished talking about this—'

'Yes, we have.' How on earth did her voice sound so casual when she was breaking up inside? 'We always knew we wanted different things, Sean. Now let's forget it. It's no big deal.'

And pigs might fly...

'Do you want to forget it?' His tone was flat and she blinked rapidly so that he wouldn't see the tears. If it wasn't so ridiculous it would be funny. Forget it? It had been the single most incredible night of her life. Never had she imagined it would be possible to feel so close to another human being. Which just went to show how false impressions could be.

'Just take me home, Sean.'

For a long moment he didn't move and she sensed that he wanted to say more, but in the end he just muttered a low curse and crunched the gears of his new car as he accelerated out of the car park.

* * *

Get up, get dressed, see patients, cook Charlie's supper, go to bed. If she just kept to that routine the days would pass. Wouldn't they?

Ally stared at the notes in front of her and they blurred as tears filled her eyes. She blinked rapidly and took a deep breath. She couldn't cry now. Not when she'd spent so long in the bathroom at home repairing the damages caused by a night of crying. She'd never worn so much make-up in her life. She spent all day lecturing herself, forcing herself to get on with the next task. Why was she being so pathetic? She'd known what she'd been doing when she'd asked him to make love to her. She'd known that Sean wasn't a for ever sort of person. So it was no good her moaning on like a wet hen.

Jack was her first patient, and she fixed a false smile on her face, hoping he wouldn't see the traces of tears.

'You're pale. Are you OK?'

Oh, great. So much for the make-up job.

'Fine,' she lied with a smile. 'Just a bit tired.'

Jack watched her for a moment and then nodded. 'Right.'

'How's the stomach?'

'Still pretty uncomfortable, to be honest.'

Ally was all brisk efficiency. This was what she needed to take her mind off Sean. Work, work and more work.

'Jack, just to be on the safe side I'm going to refer you for a gastroscopy and ask them to test for *Helicobacter pylori*.'

Jack laughed. 'What on earth is that?'

'It's a bacterium that sits in the stomach and is thought to cause ulcers in some cases,' Ally explained. 'If the test is positive then the treatment is a short course of drugs which clear it up completely.'

'Fine.' Jack nodded and Ally explained what the gastroscopy would involve and promised to refer him quickly.

Her next patient was Pete Williams, now discharged from hospital and looking well and happy.

'I came to say thanks, actually, Dr McGuire.' He perched on his chair, his brown hair tousled. 'The hospital arranged for me to have one of those tiny blood glucose meters you told me about and it's great! I don't even have to stop running when I test so I can join in with all the rest—brilliant.'

Ally smiled. 'I'm glad. And how are you feeling now, Pete?'

'Oh, I'm mended, really.' He blushed. 'I still feel like a total idiot, though.'

Ally thought of how close she and Sean had come to getting into trouble in the mountains and gave a wry smile. 'Well, don't. Everyone does something silly from time to time so don't give it another thought. I'm just glad it's turned out all right.'

She watched him go and thought that if it hadn't been for Sean, Pete would have died on the mountain that day. Sean. Wherever her thoughts turned he was there, lurking.

By clever use of her time she managed to avoid seeing him after surgery, going straight out on her calls without going near the staffroom. Noticing that the duty doctor had been called out to Kelly Watson the night before, she drove to the house and pulled up outside. It was time to get to the bottom of this.

Mrs Watson opened the door, looking tired and drained. 'Hello, Dr McGuire, come in.'

'I gather you had a bad night.' Ally followed her through to the kitchen and set her bag down on the floor. 'What happened?'

'I don't know.' Mrs Watson flicked the kettle on with shaking hands. 'She just suddenly got worse.'

Ally watched her thoughtfully. 'I must admit I'm baffled. The steroids that Kelly is taking should be controlling these attacks.'

There was a long silence and then Mrs Watson sighed, rubbing her fingers along her brow to ease the strain. 'She doesn't take them.'

So Lucy had been right. 'What do you mean, she doesn't take them?'

'You wouldn't understand…'

Ally settled herself on one of the kitchen chairs, her expression sympathetic. 'Try me.'

Mrs Watson stared at the floor for a long minute. 'It's because of my nephew. He takes steroids and they're affecting him so badly. It's awful—his growth, the shape of his face…' She sniffed. 'I don't want that happening to my Kelly.'

'Is your nephew asthmatic, too?'

'No.' Mrs Watson blew her nose and shook her head. 'No, he isn't. He's got ulcerative colitis, but steroids are steroids, aren't they?'

'Well, no, actually, they're not, but I can see why you're worried.' Ally chose her words carefully. 'The first big difference is that Kelly's steroids are inhaled, and there are fewer side effects when the drugs are taken that way.'

'But they could still affect her growth, couldn't they?'

'It's possible,' Ally said honestly, 'although I doubt it at the doses that Kelly takes. Studies have shown that untreated asthma can also affect children's growth patterns.'

Mrs Watson frowned. 'What, you mean it could affect her growth if she doesn't take them?'

Ally nodded. 'That's right. But on top of that there's the stress and fear every time she has an attack. It's frightening for all of you.'

'And you don't think the drugs will make her like my nephew?'

'No, I don't. I think what's essential here is to find just the right level of drugs to control Kelly's asthma and give her that and no more. That's the principle of good asthma management.'

Mrs Watson stared at her and then nodded slowly. 'Yes. I see that now. I've been very silly, haven't I?'

'You were worrying about Kelly and I understand that, but next time you have a fear like that come and talk it through with me.' Ally stood up and picked up her bag. 'Now, why don't you bring Kelly to our next asthma clinic and we'll start from scratch again.'

Mrs Watson nodded. 'I'll do that. Thanks, Dr McGuire.'

Ally climbed back into her car, feeling a sense of relief. Maybe now little Kelly could start living a normal life again.

After seeing a man with chest pains, whom she admitted to hospital, and a toddler with an ear infection she called in on the Thompsons.

Mary answered the door and her face brightened. 'Oh, hello, Dr McGuire. We weren't expecting you.'

'I was in the area so I thought I'd call.' Ally followed her through into the kitchen.

'Geoff's out, actually.'

Something about Mary's overly casual tone made Ally's eyes narrow. 'Anywhere nice?'

'Oh, you know…' Mary giggled nervously and flicked the switch on the kettle. 'Would you join me for a coffee?'

'I'd love one,' Ally said honestly. She'd skipped having one at the surgery because she hadn't wanted to bump into Sean. 'So how are things?'

'Fine,' Mary said with a bright smile, and then she met Ally's eyes and her smile faded. 'No, they're not fine, actually.'

'Is he drinking again?' Ally's voice was gentle but Mary shook her head.

'No. Well, at least he certainly isn't at home.' She frowned and thought for a moment. 'No, I know he isn't. I've lived with it for long enough. I'd recognise the signs.'

'So what's worrying you?' Ally took the mug of coffee Mary offered but declined a biscuit. 'Thanks.'

Mary sagged onto one of the kitchen stools, her face tired and pale. 'He just doesn't seem himself.'

'In what way?'

Mary stared into her coffee. 'Well, he's very flat. My Geoff's always the life and soul of the party, you know? Even through all this he's managed to put a brave face on it for most of the time. ''We'll sort all this out, Mary,'' he keeps saying, but the last few days…'

'Is he sleeping?'

Mary shook her head. 'No. He waits until he thinks I'm asleep and then he gets up and comes down here. I've heard him pacing around at four in the morning, but he always denies it when I try and talk to him.'

Ally took a sip of coffee. 'Does he seem depressed to you?'

'Yes, I suppose he does.' Mary stared at her bleakly. 'He's a very proud man, Dr McGuire, and this has wrecked his confidence in himself. He thinks that everyone is talking about him, laughing—you know? It was that wretched newspaper article that did it. Before then it was our private problem but now the whole world knows.'

Ally reached across the kitchen table and squeezed her hand. 'Well, you know as well as I do that the world isn't interested for more than a day. He's yesterday's news, Mary—but I don't suppose that's any consolation to him.'

'No.'

'He's due to come and see me this week—do you think he will?'

Mary shrugged. 'I don't know. He's very independent. Doesn't like asking for help. It was different when he was so badly affected by the alcohol, but now he thinks it's up to him to snap out of it.'

Ally frowned. 'Well, it won't be that easy.'

'Try telling him that.' Mary stared down at her empty coffee-cup. 'I don't know what to do. I'm at my wit's end, frankly.'

'If he doesn't come and see me in surgery I'll call and see him here,' Ally promised, standing up and picking up her bag.

'Thanks, Dr McGuire.' Mary gave her a tired smile and showed her to the door.

By considerable effort on her part Ally managed to avoid Sean for most of the week, but there was no escape on Friday when she pulled up outside the barn and saw him standing with Charlie, staring at the fells.

'Hero's gone, Mum.'

Ally locked the car door, avoiding Sean's penetrating gaze.

'What do you mean, he's gone? Where's Grandma?' Why was Sean looking after her child instead of her mother?

'Someone on the farm broke his arm and Grandma had to go, so Sean said he'd stay with me.' Charlie's face was blotched with tears and she was clutching Sean's hand. 'Hero was playing in the garden but he jumped the fence again and he hasn't been back all afternoon.'

Ally slipped her arms round her daughter and gave her a hug. 'He won't come to any harm, sweetheart. He's probably just gone for a walk. He'll come back.'

'But it's snowed!' Charlie's face was anxious and Ally kissed her and then stood up.

'He's got fur, darling. Fur keeps him warm.'

Charlie stared across the fields. 'Sean says he'll go and look for him.'

Ally's mouth tightened and her chin lifted slightly. 'Sean's busy, darling. Hero will find his own way home. He's done it before.'

'Yes, but not when it's snowed.' Charlie tugged at her arm. 'Can't Sean go and look, Mummy?'

Ally gritted her teeth. 'No, sweetheart. Sean's got other things to do. Now, you and I are going to cook some dinner and Sean has to go home.'

Sean dropped down to Charlie's level, his dark eyes gentle. 'I'll tell you what—you make dinner with your mum, and if he hasn't come home by the time you go to bed then you give me a shout and I'll take a look.'

'That won't be necessary.' Ally gave him a cool smile, careful not to look at the hard line of his jaw, that firm mouth or the breadth of his shoulders. It was all too painful...

She hurried Charlie indoors and spent the evening playing with her daughter and doing one chore after another. Every corner of the barn gleamed as she dusted and cleaned, and a delicious smell of casserole wafted out of the kitchen. Just as she was laying the table for supper she heard Hero bark.

Relief washed over her as she called to her daughter. 'There you are, darling, he's home.'

'Oh, Mum!' Charlie leapt from her stool and dashed to the front door, falling on the dog who stood there wagging his tail.

Ally dried him off, settled Charlie into bed and had a quick bath herself, wrapping her wet hair in a towel before returning to the living room where the dog was sprawled in front of the blazing fire.

'You're in big trouble, mate,' she muttered, taking a handful of fur and pulling it gently.

Hero whined and stuck his nose in her hand. The whine turned to a growl and he barked as someone rapped on the door.

Ally froze. Sean, of course. Well, she could hardly ignore it, could she? At least she'd pulled her jeans back on after her bath, instead of getting ready for bed.

Pulling herself together, she padded across the wooden floor and jerked open the front door.

'Is he back?' Sean came straight to the point and she nodded.

'Half an hour ago. Thanks for looking after Charlie…' She gave him a polite smile and went to close the door, but he was too quick for her, planting a foot in the door and shouldering his way past her.

'I've let you avoid me for a week. That's long enough.'

Her heart galloped uncontrollably and she gripped the doorhandle. 'I'm not avoiding you, I just—'

'Close the door, Ally, you're letting out the heat.' His expression was grim. She hesitated and did as he ordered.

'I think Geoff Thompson might be depressed.' Maybe if she kept the conversation professional she could avoid having to talk about more painful things. Like the fact he didn't love her and never would. 'Mary says he's—'

'I don't give a damn about the Thompsons. I want to talk about us.'

His legs were planted firmly apart in a gesture of pure male domination and she wrapped her arms round her body and gave a little shiver. It was because she'd just come out of the bath, of course. 'There is no us.'

'There was on Saturday night,' he said with brutal frankness, and she turned her head away so that she didn't have to look at him, the sudden action loosening the towel around her head. Her damp hair fell in soft waves around her shoulders and she heard the hiss of his indrawn breath.

'For goodness' sake, Ally, I don't understand what this is all about.' He closed his hands over her shoulders and pulled her towards him. 'I didn't force you...'

'No.' She gave a shake of her head, her eyes bleak. 'No, you didn't force me.'

'I know I hurt you and I'm sorry. Is that what's wrong?' His voice was rough and she coloured at the intimacy of his question.

'No. You were—' Her throat clogged and she coughed. Oh, hell! 'It was fine.'

'Fine?' He gave her a little shake. 'Fine?'

'Oh, what do you want me to say?' Suddenly she was shouting at him. 'It was fantastic. It was the single most wonderful thing that has ever happened in my life—there, are you satisfied now?'

He looked totally baffled. 'So why are you avoiding me?'

Her anger dissipated and she felt suddenly tired. 'Because you wish it had never happened.'

His hands fell to his sides and a muscle worked in his cheek. 'That's not true.'

She jerked away from him, the towel around her shoulders sliding to the floor. 'It is true, Sean, and we both know it. Let's be honest here for five minutes, shall we? I love you. I love you with every bone in my body...' She saw him tense slightly and gave a short laugh. 'Oh, I know you don't want to hear that, but it's the truth, and if you really want to know why I'm avoiding you then you'd better hear the truth—and the truth is, we don't want the same thing.'

He was frowning. 'I never wanted a one-night stand.'

'Oh?' Her eyes were bright with tears. 'So you wouldn't have minded second helpings?'

'Dammit, it wasn't like that and you know it.' His dark eyes were alight with anger and suddenly she sagged, the fight gone. She just wanted him to go, too.

'Forget it, Sean. You've made your position more than clear.'

His expression was grim. 'This isn't about me.'

'No, of course it isn't.' Ally used sarcasm to hide her pain. 'It's never about you, is it, Sean? You don't talk about your past, you don't open up to anyone, you don't trust anyone, you don't expose your feelings to anyone—'

His hands were clenched by his sides. 'Have you finished?'

'Actually, no.' She stared at him calmly. In a minute she was going to burst into tears and make a total fool of herself, but first there were things she needed to get off her chest. 'You accused me of being afraid to take a risk, but what about you, Sean? Do you take risks? Do you allow yourself to get close to anyone, to develop a relationship? No, you don't. Because you just might fall in love and that would cause all sorts of complications, wouldn't it? And God forbid that you should ever have children because you're afraid that loving them will make you vulnerable, too—'

His eyes were full of pain. 'Dammit, Ally—'

'Well, let me tell you one more thing, Sean Nicholson.' Her voice cracked slightly and she took a deep breath. 'As you once pointed out to me, there are no guarantees in life. The best you can do is to have hope and trust people. And you know what? Being a parent *does* make you vulnerable, because suddenly there's someone in your life that matters more than yourself. Parenthood is all about exposing yourself to hurt, and it's tough. Really tough. But that doesn't mean people give up on it. Very few people are like your mother, Sean.'

His face was white. 'You don't understand.'

Ally stared at him sadly, all her anger suddenly gone. 'No, I suppose I don't, really, because you've never trusted me enough to explain. And that's why this relationship is never going anywhere. I thought I could take whatever you were prepared to give, but it isn't enough.'

He stared at her for a long moment, a muscle working in his cheek. 'You're saying you want me to marry you?'

'Because you're the first man I've ever been to bed with?' She gave a short laugh. 'Don't be ridiculous, Sean. I don't care about marriage—but I do care about commitment. I can't have a relationship with a man who bails out before he gets emotionally involved. I thought I could, but I can't.'

His whole body was rigid with tension. 'So that's that, then?'

'It would seem so.'

Why didn't he argue with her, dammit? Tell her he loved her madly. Tell her everything he was thinking and feeling? But he didn't.

The tears were going to come at any moment. If he didn't leave soon she'd make an utter fool of herself.

He stood for a long moment just staring at her, his eyes tormented, and for a wild moment she thought he was going to kiss her. But then his hands clenched into fists and he walked away from her, wrenching open the front door and slamming it behind him.

CHAPTER NINE

THE next week was a nightmare.

Every time Ally turned round she seemed to fall over Sean, her only consolation being that he seemed to look as drawn and strained as she felt. She couldn't sleep, she didn't eat and then, to cap it all, she went down with a stomach bug that seemed to be affecting most of Cumbria.

On the third day she felt slightly better and dragged herself into work, ignoring the feeling of nausea that gnawed away in her stomach. She hadn't actually vomited for two days so she should be fine to work. Anyway, one of the other partners was off with the same thing so she really needed to be there, helping.

Will didn't think so. 'It's hardly a good advertisement for the practice if the doctors look as though they're at death's door. Go back to bed.'

Ally shook her head. 'I'm fine now. I just feel a bit feeble.' And exhausted. Totally drained. Like a puppet with its strings cut. But if she sat down she'd be OK.

Will was watching her closely. 'This is more than a stomach bug.'

'Don't be ridiculous.' Ally avoided his searching gaze and sorted out her desk. 'Everyone's got it.'

'Agreed—but it lasts twenty-four hours and then they're as right as rain.'

Ally rummaged in her drawer. 'I'm as right as rain.'

'It's Sean, isn't it?'

Her hand stilled and she gritted her teeth. She wasn't going to break down. Not here, with a surgery to run.

'I'm fine, Will.'

There was a moment's silence. 'Well, I'm really sorry, and if there's anything I can do just ask.'

The kindness in his voice brought tears to the surface. 'Thanks, Will.'

Fortunately Will had the wisdom to leave her alone then, giving her time to pull herself together before surgery. But as she buzzed for the first patient, something he'd said nagged in her brain. The stomach bug only lasted for twenty-four hours— so why was she still feeling sick?

She went through surgery on automatic, looking in ears and throats, listening to chests, writing prescriptions for antibiotics and seeing more people with the stomach bug, and as her last patient shut the door behind her she reached for the calendar, her hands shaking.

Carefully she counted the days, then checked again and closed her eyes. Dear God, her period was late and in all the stress she hadn't even noticed. How could she not have noticed? She'd been due the night she and Sean had made love, which was why she'd thought she'd been safe. For a moment she sat and stared at the calendar, totally numb, and then a flame of excitement sparked inside her.

A baby. Sean's baby.

She put the calendar down on her desk and stared out of the window at the mountains, a smile starting on her face. What was the matter with her? She should have been feeling horrified! She was expecting a baby by a man who didn't want children or commitment. So why was she smiling?

She placed a hand over her abdomen in an instinctively protective gesture. Because it was part of Sean. Part of her love for him. There was no question of her not keeping it. The only question was what to do about Sean...

Her smile faded. He didn't ever want children, he'd made that clear enough, and he didn't want her either—not long term, at least. As she stared out of the window she saw that it had started to snow heavily and suddenly she felt more peaceful. She'd survive. Of course she would. And she wouldn't tell

Sean about the baby. What was the point? He didn't want her and he'd made it clear that he didn't want a child. She'd manage with the help of her family and friends. After all, she'd managed with Charlie…

It snowed heavily for another three days and most of Cumbria was paralysed.

'Nothing's moving on the roads, but the patients still seem to manage to turn up for surgery,' Helen grumbled, checking the appointments to try and squeeze in another extra.

Ally gave her a wan smile. 'I expect they're bored so they want to come and see us.'

'Yes, well, I wish they'd—' Helen had glanced up and stopped in mid-sentence. 'Ally, are you all right? You look dreadful!'

'Thanks.' Ally gave her a wry grin. 'You know how to make someone feel better, I'll say that for you. Any extras for me?'

'Two more with the stomach bug,' Helen told her, her eyes reflecting her concern. 'Do you want Will or Sean to see them?'

'No!' Ally took a deep breath and picked up the notes. 'I'll see them. Send the first one in, will you, Helen?'

She settled herself in her consulting room, wondering whether she'd survive three months of nausea. She thought back to the number of times she'd glibly told patients that it would pass in time, and vowed never to be so dismissive again. She felt ill, totally drained of energy and exhausted, and sooner or later she was going to have to think of a new excuse because the 'stomach bug' routine was wearing thin.

She forced herself to concentrate as her first extra of the morning tapped on the door, another victim of the stomach bug. After examining him and giving him advice on rehydration and managing diarrhoea, Ally showed him out and then suddenly lifted her hand to her throat. She was going to be sick. She made it to the staff toilet just in time, and when she staggered out ten minutes later she found Sean standing there, his expression grim.

'Helen told me you still aren't well.'

Oh, not now! She just wasn't up to a confrontation. 'I'm fine, Sean.'

'You look it!' His wry tone made her shrug ruefully.

'I've just picked up the same bug everyone else has.'

He stared at her for a long moment, his gaze measuring. 'Except that everyone else seems to have recovered in half the time.' There was a strange light in his eyes and for a brief moment of panic Ally wondered if he'd guessed.

'Dr McGuire!' The urgency of Helen's voice carried down the corridor and Ally breathed a sigh of relief, excused herself and walked briskly to Reception.

'What's the matter?'

Helen was just replacing the receiver, her expression worried. 'That was Felicity Webster. She's gone into labour and there's no way she can get to hospital in time. The roads are impassable and she's contracting every two minutes. She's in a total panic.'

'Where's the midwife?' Ally was picking up her coat even as she asked the question.

'Stuck with a woman in premature labour the other side of the Kirkstone pass.'

'You can't go—you're not well.' Sean picked up his bag and made for the door.

'Wait!' Ally caught up with him, her expression determined. 'Of course I'm going—she's my patient.'

'Well, you're not going on your own!' He stared at her and then gave a wry smile. 'I'm starting to learn how stubborn you are, so shall we compromise for once? We'll both go.'

Ally frowned as he jangled a set of keys. 'You won't get through in your car.'

'Will's already lent me his four-wheel drive for my calls.' Sean shrugged on a heavy jacket. 'Are you sure you're up to this?'

She nodded, wrapping a scarf around her neck and pushing

her hands into her pockets. 'Absolutely. I wouldn't miss it for the world. I love delivering babies.'

He gave a short laugh. 'I'm glad one of us does because it's certainly not my strong point.'

Ally followed him out to Will's Range Rover, relieved to sit down. She felt awful. What would happen if she felt like this for the whole nine months?

All along the road to Felicity's they passed abandoned vehicles, some strewn haphazardly across the road where their drivers had obviously become stuck in the snow and slush. The snow was worse as they approached Felicity's, but Sean handled Will's vehicle with enviable ease, negotiating patches of ice and heavy slush in his usual cool manner.

Felicity's husband was standing in the doorway when they arrived, waving his arms frantically.

'Is he a panicker or is she delivering?' Sean switched off the engine and they both hurried down the path.

Hugh greeted them with relief. 'She's pushing!'

'Well, tell her to try not to, Hugh!' Ally elbowed her way past Sean and took the stairs two at a time, forgetting how exhausted she felt.

Felicity was crouched on the floor at the foot of the bed, her hair tangled and her face blotched with crying.

'Oh, Dr McGuire, thank goodness you're here. I've been so scared…after the awful time I had with the others.'

'Everything will be just fine, Felicity,' Ally soothed gently, stroking her patient's hair and giving her shoulders a quick squeeze. 'You've had an excellent pregnancy and there's no reason why this birth shouldn't be the nicest, calmest experience you've ever had. Now then, I need to examine you so let's get you back on the bed.'

With Hugh and Sean helping, she manoeuvred Felicity onto the bed. Ally then scrubbed her hands and snapped on a pair of sterile gloves.

'OK, let's take a look.' With infinite care she examined Felicity, discovering that the cervix was fully dilated.

'Oh, that hurts so much!' Felicity screwed up her face and Ally finished her examination, tugging off the gloves and giving the labouring woman a smile.

'Well, this baby isn't hanging around!' She glanced at Sean, who was looking tense and edgy.

'Can you open the delivery pack, Dr Nicholson, and draw up the Syntometrine?' She turned to Felicity's husband. 'Hugh, can you fetch some candles and play a tape with something really soothing on it—any Schubert string quartets?'

Hugh gaped at her. 'Well, yes, actually, but—'

'Great.' Ally rearranged the pillows and made Felicity comfortable. 'Fetch them, will you? Now, Felicity, you can lie down if you like, but you might find it easier to go back on the floor where you were and squat. What do you think?'

Felicity clutched her hand. 'I don't know. I just think it's all going so wrong.'

Ally slipped her arm round her patient's shoulders and gave her a hug. 'It's not going wrong at all, Felicity. It's perfect. Trust me.'

Felicity gave her a wobbly smile and allowed them to help her back onto the floor.

'Pass me some of those towels, Hugh,' Ally ordered, spreading them carefully beneath Felicity. 'That's it. There. Now, doesn't the room look nice with those candles?'

It did. Warm and calm, and suddenly Felicity seemed to relax. 'I've got another contraction coming.'

Ally snapped on a fresh pair of gloves. 'OK, push down with the pain. That's it. Good girl. I can see the head, Felicity. Lots of dark hair.'

'Ooh...' Felicity groaned and reached out for Hugh.

'Stand behind her and support her under her arms,' Ally suggested, and he did just that, holding her while she laboured.

'Will it be all right like this?' Felicity made a noise somewhere between a moan and a giggle. 'I don't want it to bang its head when it's born.'

Ally laughed. 'I've got my fishing net ready. It'll be fine.'

She glanced up and caught Sean watching her, an odd expression on his face. With a soft smile she handed him the suction tube.

'Can you clear the baby's mouth and nose?'

He nodded and watched while she applied gentle pressure on the perineum with one hand, while placing her other hand on the head of the infant to control the rate of delivery.

The head slid out neatly, and emotion clogged her throat. It was so amazing, the birth of a baby. And she was going to have one of her own. She was going to have Sean's baby. She blinked rapidly. But he'd never know. He didn't want to know.

Sean cleared the baby's airways and while they waited for the next contraction Ally rested her eyes on his hard, male features, memorising every line and angle of his handsome face. He glanced up to reassure Felicity and frowned as he caught her looking at him, his eyes suddenly questioning as he read the obvious yearning in her eyes.

Instantly she looked away, swallowing hard to subdue her feelings. Oh, help! Had she given it all away?

Felicity groaned. 'I've got another one coming...'

'OK, pant for me. That's it.' With gentle skill Ally delivered the anterior shoulder, aware of Sean giving the injection which would make the uterus contract. The rest of the baby followed, the cord was cut, and she lifted the infant gently into Felicity's arms.

'Oh, Hugh! Oh— I...' Felicity burst into tears and Ally blinked rapidly to clear her own eyes.

'Congratulations.' Her voice was husky. 'A little girl.'

'Oh, Mummy loves you, darling.' Felicity cuddled the bawling bundle close and sobbed quietly, while the tears streamed down Hugh's cheeks.

Ally glanced up at Sean, but his face was like a mask, his expression totally unreadable as he cleared up some of the equipment they'd used.

Didn't he feel anything? How could anyone see a baby born and not be moved?

Lost in her own thoughts, she applied traction to the placenta, which was delivered easily, and then checked that it was complete.

By the time they'd cleaned Felicity up and settled her in bed to feed her new daughter, the midwife arrived with wet feet and frozen hands.

'Gosh, it's lovely and warm in here.' She stood in front of the extra fire Hugh had thought to put in the room for the birth of the baby. 'You look great!'

Felicity gave her a euphoric smile. 'I am. It was incredible. Nothing like either of my previous deliveries. I enjoyed it. I really did.'

Ally laughed and cleared up the last of her mess. 'Thank goodness! I wouldn't have fancied using forceps or the ventouse at home!' She carefully wrote down all the details of the delivery, handed them over to the midwife and promised to call on Felicity again the next day.

'There's no point at all in you struggling into hospital in this weather when you're both so fit. If you've got any worries at all just give me a ring.' As an afterthought she scribbled down her home number. 'Call me at home if you need to.'

Felicity looked at her gratefully, her eyes misty. 'I don't know what to say, how to thank you…'

'No need.' Ally's voice was gruff as she picked up her bag. 'Well, we'll leave you in peace now.'

She picked her way through the snow back to the Range Rover and shivered while Sean unlocked the door.

'You were great.' He slammed the door and turned the key in the ignition, his breath clouding the freezing air. 'I wouldn't have been able to do that without you.'

Ally glanced at him in surprise and then huddled deeper into her coat. 'Of course you could. You've delivered babies before.'

He gave a grim smile, his hands holding the wheel steady as the vehicle lurched through the snow.

'It's not the technical bit that's a problem, it's all the emotional stuff.'

'Like what?'

He stared straight ahead, his jaw tense. 'I don't know. One minute she's panicking, then she's screaming in agony, then she's laughing. However she was reacting, you were one step ahead of her—I just couldn't do that.'

'And, I couldn't put in a chest drain at an altitude of nine hundred metres in a howling blizzard,' Ally said quietly. 'We all have different skills.'

'Maybe.' He cleared his throat, his voice gruff. 'You're a very warm, compassionate person, Ally McGuire. Whatever you're doing, you give your whole self. You don't hold anything back, do you?'

She looked at his hard profile and felt a lump in her throat. 'Not with people I trust. But I suppose I've been lucky. I've always had family who love me.'

For a moment she thought he was going to say something more, but his eyes were suddenly distant and he pulled into the drive without another word, leaving her with her own thoughts.

Geoff Thompson didn't turn up for his next appointment and Ally made a call to the community alcohol team, but they were quite happy with his progress.

'I think he's probably depressed,' she confided in Will one morning, and he nodded.

'Very likely, in the circumstances. Does he seem depressed?'

'Well, not at first, but ever since we finished the detox programme he's been avoiding me.' Ally frowned. 'I've called at his home twice but he's always out.'

Will rubbed his chin thoughtfully. 'Well, he's been through a great deal so I wouldn't be surprised if he's depressed.'

Ally made a note to call at his home again, trying to ignore the sudden wave of nausea that hit her.

Jack came in to see her later that morning, and she told him that his gastroscopy had shown a small ulcer, but nothing more sinister. 'But you tested positive for *H. pylori* so I need to give you some drugs to clear it up.'

Jack raised an eyebrow. 'And that should do the trick?'

Ally nodded. 'Absolutely. You take three drugs together—an ulcer preparation and two different antibiotics—and that should eradicate the organism that causes the ulcer.'

She tapped keys on the computer and printed out a prescription, which she handed to him.

'I hear you were called out yesterday?'

'Yes.' Jack took the prescription and tucked it in his pocket. 'A woman with a sprained ankle halfway up Harrison Stickle. If I had a fiver for every female with a sprained ankle I've seen this year, I could stop doing the lottery.'

Ally laughed. 'Any excuse to ogle.'

'She was sixty, Ally,' Jack said dryly, shrugging on his jacket, 'although why a woman of her age wanted to walk in the fells in early December is a mystery to me. But there you are. It's the likes of her that keep me fit.'

They talked for a few minutes more and then she followed him out, picking up her list of house calls from Helen.

Making a note to add Felicity Webster and Geoff Thompson to the list, she wrapped herself up in her woolly coat and took the keys to the four-wheel drive. Since the snow had started they'd worked the calls so that the one with the calls further afield took the Range Rover.

She called on a man with chest pains first and decided he had indigestion. Then she saw an old lady who'd slipped on the ice and hurt her leg. Examining her gently, she noted that the right leg was shortened and externally rotated. Fractured neck of femur.

'You've broken your hip, Mrs Wise,' she told her gently, exchanging looks with the woman's daughter who was hovering in the background.

'Oh, dear. Does that mean a trip to hospital?'

'I'm afraid so.' Ally covered her with a blanket and called an ambulance, waiting with them until it arrived.

Next on her list was Felicity, now three days post-delivery and thriving.

'She's such a guzzler!' Felicity patted her daughter on the back to wind her, and Ally smiled.

'How are the children taking it?'

'Oh, they keep poking her.' Felicity laughed and latched the baby on the breast again. 'If she survives until Christmas it will be a miracle.'

'And how are you?'

'Oh, absolutely fine, thanks to you.' Felicity glanced up, her expression grateful, and Ally smiled.

'You did it, Felicity, not me.'

Felicity shook her head, settling the baby more comfortably on her arm. 'No. I was in a total panic. I had such a bad time with the others.'

'Well, I'm glad it all worked out so well.' Ally checked the position of the uterus and then said goodbye, checking that she'd finished her calls before she made her way to the Thompsons. If she did catch Geoff Thompson in, she didn't want to have to dash off in a hurry to do another call.

The Thompsons' house looked totally deserted. She rapped on the door twice and squinted up at the windows, but there were no signs of life. Well, they could be anywhere, she reasoned, climbing back in the Range Rover and driving back to the surgery.

Suddenly she felt hideously sick and sat still, trying to fight the waves of nausea and faintness which swamped her. She was breathing steadily with her eyes closed in an attempt to control it when the door was tugged open.

Sean stood there, his dark brows clashing in a frown. 'What's the matter? Are you ill again?'

'No. Yes—maybe a bit.' Help! She had to give some excuse for the way she felt. 'I just feel a bit weedy, that's all.'

He stared at her for a long moment. 'It's been a week and a half, Ally. The bug doesn't last that long.'

He knew. She could tell by the look in his eyes. He'd guessed.

'Maybe it's not the same bug.' Her protest was half-hearted and he gave her a grim smile.

'I think you and I had better have a talk, don't you?'

'Not now, Sean.' She tugged the keys out of the ignition and took another deep breath to try and control the nausea.

'Yes, *now*.' He jerked open the door and stood waiting while she gathered up her bag and coat and slid to the ground. Her legs gave way under her and she would have gone all the way if he hadn't caught her.

'Steady...' He stiffened slightly and she reminded herself that she wasn't allowed the luxury of leaning on this man any more. Pulling herself together, she walked towards the health centre with as much composure as she could muster. Once inside he caught her wrist and propelled her through to his room. She stood just inside the door, watching him warily.

'You're pregnant, aren't you?' His face was set and grim and her heart seemed to drop into her stomach.

'Sean, I—'

'When were you going to tell me?'

His expression was forbidding and she slipped a hand onto her abdomen in an instinctively protective gesture.

'I don't know. I...'

He was suddenly pale, his eyes cold and distant as if he were talking to a stranger. As if the love-making between them had never happened. 'It's the oldest trick in the book, isn't it?'

She frowned, baffled. 'Trick? What do you mean, trick?'

'To get me to marry you.' He strode over to the window, staring out across the fells.

She stared at his broad back, stunned. 'You think I did it on purpose to get you to marry me?'

He shrugged, his expression challenging as he turned to look at her. 'Well, didn't you?'

'No!' Her blue eyes were wide, her expression horrified, as she shook her head. 'No. Of course I didn't.'

'Why are you pregnant, then?'

She stared at him, bemused. 'Sean, it was an accident...'

He smiled wryly and shrugged those wide shoulders. 'You're a GP, Ally. You know the facts of life. I remember asking you if you were protected.'

She coloured hotly and swallowed. 'I was. I mean, it shouldn't have happened. It was totally the wrong time of the month.'

'Obviously.' There was no missing the irony in his voice and tears pricked her eyes.

'How can you possibly think I did it on purpose after everything you've said about not wanting children?'

'I don't know. Perhaps because you seemed determined to reform me.' He gave a humourless laugh. 'Get pregnant and then I'll be forced to stick around and make a commitment.'

Ally shook her head, numb with disbelief. 'I'm not forcing you to do anything—'

Sean's eyes blazed with anger. 'Aren't you? You say you know how I feel about not having children, about letting them down. Well, if you know all that how come you're standing there telling me you're pregnant?'

'It was an accident...'

He swore under his breath. 'And pigs might fly.'

'Oh, for goodness' sake!' She stared at him helplessly. 'How can I prove it to you?'

He gave a short laugh and looked at her, his eyes bleak. 'Well, that's the beauty of this situation isn't it? You can't.'

'If you trusted me...'

'Why should I trust you?'

She swallowed hard. 'Because I love you and I would never do anything to hurt you.'

His jaw tightened. 'You just have.'

'No.' She shook her head slowly, trying to understand the way he was feeling, the reason he was reacting so violently. 'You're scared that I've trapped you into marriage—'

He made a dismissive gesture. 'I'm not scared!'

'Yes, you are.' She stood her ground, resisting the temptation to back away when she met the full anger of his gaze. 'You're scared of commitment and that you're going to have to marry me, but you're not, Sean.'

He turned away from her so that she couldn't see his expression. 'You haven't left me much choice, have you?'

'Sean, I wouldn't marry you if you were the last man on earth!' The words spilled out and she blinked back the tears that threatened to follow. 'I don't want to marry someone who isn't capable of giving love to me and my baby.'

He turned to face her, his expression grim. 'Don't you mean "our" baby?'

'No.' She choked on the word and shook her head. 'I don't mean "our" baby. It's not "our" baby, Sean, because you don't want it. It's my baby, and mine alone.'

His jaw clenched. 'You're going to keep it, then?'

She stared at him in horror. 'You're not asking me to—?'

'Dammit, no!' He interrupted her roughly, leaning on the back of a chair and sucking the breath through his teeth. 'No. Not that. But there are other options. It's not as if it was planned. It'll totally change your life.'

'I know how much babies change your life. I've got Charlie, remember?' She lifted her chin and held his gaze. 'This is my baby and I'm going to love it with every bone in my body, so if you're suggesting adoption you can forget that, too. I would never give my baby to anyone else.'

'You don't know that.' His knuckles were white as he gripped the chair-back. 'If the going gets tough you just might bail out…'

What was he talking about? 'What do you mean, bail out? I can't bail out. I'm its mother!'

His hard mouth twisted. 'You wouldn't be the first. Babies can be hard work. What if it cries a lot?'

Was he talking about his own mother? Was that what this was all about? How could she convince him? How could she ever get this man to trust anyone ever again? If she'd met his mother in the street she would have thumped her, along with the foster-parents who'd obviously done nothing to win a young boy's trust.

'You think I'd give it to someone else if it cried? If it was less than perfect? That's not me, Sean.' She stared at him, aghast, love and compassion for him swamping her own feelings of misery. 'You really don't know me at all, do you? I don't need this baby shrinkwrapped with a guarantee attached. This baby can cry every night for ten years if it wants to. I'll still love it and care for it.'

'On your own…' His voice was hoarse.

She shook her head. 'No. Not on my own. I've got my parents and my brothers and Charlie.' She met his gaze head on. 'This baby will be surrounded by people who will love and protect him. You can be sure of that. He'll have everything he needs.'

'Except a father.'

She swallowed hard. 'Yes.'

There was a long silence and she could hear his ragged breathing. 'And if I did ask you to marry me?'

'The answer would still be no, Sean.' The strain of the encounter had stripped away the last of her energy, and she sagged slightly. 'No, I wouldn't marry you. You'd always accuse me of having blackmailed you, and I couldn't live with that.'

And before she made a total fool of herself she turned on her heel and walked out of the room, closing the door quietly behind her.

CHAPTER TEN

ALLY lay in her bed and stared up at the ceiling. She couldn't sleep. All she could think about was Sean and what he'd said about the baby. Did he really think she'd consider having it adopted? Her blood boiled when she thought of Sean's mother. What sort of a woman was she to have let her own flesh and blood go into foster-care? No wonder he was so afraid to love anyone. From the sound of it, he'd never had any constancy in his life. Apart from Will and Molly, of course, but maybe they'd come on the scene too late to influence his ability to trust anyone.

With an impatient sound she sat up in bed, scraping her blonde hair away from her face with slim fingers. She was never going to be able to sleep. Never. Reaching for her dressing-gown, she pulled it on and fastened it around her waist. If she wasn't going to be able to sleep she may as well go and have a drink.

Padding into the kitchen, she flicked on the light and took a bottle of milk out of the fridge.

Just as she reached for a mug the phone rang.

One glance at the clock on the oven told her it was two in the morning. Who on earth was ringing at this time? She wasn't on call.

'Hello?'

It was Jack, his voice grim and serious as he got straight to the point. 'Geoff Thompson is your patient, isn't he?'

'Geoff?' Ally frowned and put the empty mug down on the table. 'Well, yes, he is. Why?'

'Because he was spotted walking into the Langdales this morning and hasn't been seen since. His wife's called the police and someone thinks they might have spotted him up by Stickle Tarn.'

'Oh, no!' Ally's face paled and she bit her lip. 'Well, don't go anywhere without me, Jack.'

'I was hoping you'd say that. Can you get your mum to stay with Charlie?'

Ally was already wriggling out of her dressing-gown. 'No problem. She can be here in ten minutes.'

'I've called out the team and the police have already called Howard, the SARDA co-ordinator.'

Ally knew that in this weather the skill of the dogs in tracking a missing person was crucial.

'I'll meet you at Dungeon Ghyll in twenty minutes.'

'Fine. Sean can give you a lift.'

Ally swallowed. 'Is he coming, too?'

'Too right.' Jack gave a short laugh. 'He's got skills we might need.'

She bowed to the inevitable and was ready and dressed in all her gear when a knock came fifteen minutes later.

Quickly she let her mother in and gave Sean, who was with her, a brief nod before making for his car.

He drove as quickly as was safe on the gritted roads, but already the snow was falling heavily, swirling into the headlights and reducing visibility.

'I should have guessed.' Ally stared into the darkness, her face strained. 'I should have guessed he might do something like this.'

Sean cursed as the car slewed across the road, turning into the skid and regaining control with admirable skill.

'Don't be ridiculous. You're not clairvoyant.' His eyes were fixed on the road, his face a mask of concentration as he battled with the awful driving conditions.

'But I suspected he was depressed.' Ally sighed and fastened her blonde hair securely, before tugging a woolly hat over her head.

Sean frowned and slowed down as they approached a junction, even though there was no traffic on the roads.

'Forget it, Ally. You're not responsible.'

Ally stared at his hard profile. 'He'll die of hypothermia if we don't get to him soon.'

Sean's mouth tightened and he eased the car up a gear. 'Well, then, let's hope we do.'

He pulled in to the car park and yanked on the handbrake, his breathing unsteady as he stared straight ahead. 'Ally, I want you to wait here.'

Ally glanced at him in surprise. 'What do you mean?'

'The weather's filthy.' Sean turned to look at her and she saw the lines of strain around his dark eyes. 'I don't want you out there on a night like this.'

Her heart stumbled. He must care about her—surely, he must—then her shoulders sagged slightly and she pulled herself together. Of course he didn't. He'd made that clear enough already. He was just too much of an original male chauvinist to recognise that she was capable of being part of the rescue team.

'He's my patient, Sean,' she said quietly. 'I have to go.'

She reached for the doorhandle but his hand closed over hers, his fingers biting into her flesh.

'Dammit, no, Ally!' His voice was urgent and there was a flash of something that looked like panic in his eyes. 'I'm asking you not to. It isn't safe.'

Ally gave him a wry smile. 'Wasn't this where we came in?'

He stared at her for a moment and his mouth twisted. 'I suppose it was.'

'You admitted you were wrong last time.'

'Only under duress—because you called me a chauvinist.' He shook his head and sat back in his seat, his eyes bleak and strained. 'I'll never be comfortable with you roaming the mountains on your own.'

'Because I'm a woman?'

His eyes held hers for a long moment and he shook his head. 'No. Not just because of that.'

Her heart thumped. 'Why, then?'

He opened his mouth and closed it again, rubbing his temples with long fingers. 'Oh, hell! I don't know. I don't know what I think any more. I just know I can't let you do it.'

'Why not, Sean?' Her voice was urgent and her eyes begged him to say it. To say that he didn't want her to go because he cared about her. Loved her.

'Dammit, Ally!' He swallowed, emotions chasing each other across his hard, male features. Then he took a deep breath and his eyes searched hers. 'You know how hard this is for me—'

The door of the car was wrenched open and Jack stood there.

'Are you two going to sit in here gossiping all night or are you coming?'

Brilliant! Full marks for timing. Ally gritted her teeth and managed to smile at Jack—just.

'We're coming. What's the plan?' Tearing her eyes away from Sean, Ally swung her legs out of the car and shivered as the freezing air folded itself around her.

Jack gathered the whole team together for a final briefing and Ally tried to concentrate on what was being said and not on the fact that Sean was standing conspicuously close to her.

As they set off up the mountain she glanced at him questioningly. 'Are you going to hold my hand all the way up in case I trip?'

He didn't laugh, his features strained and taut. 'If I could stop you going I would.'

'I'll be fine, Sean.'

'Too right you will—' his voice was a low growl '—because you'll have me breathing down your neck.'

The thought warmed her insides and for a brief moment she allowed herself the luxury of pretending it was because he really cared. Gazing at those powerful shoulders, she felt her heart flip and a lump form in her throat. She loved him so much. For a brief moment her hand covered their baby. He saw the gesture, his eyes lifting to hers.

Then the moment passed and they were tramping up the mountain at a steady pace behind the rest of the mountain rescue team in search of Geoff Thompson, their torches cutting through the darkness and the swirling snow.

It was Red, Lucy's search dog, that found Geoff nearly three hours later when they'd almost given up hope. Barking to indicate what she'd found, the dog stood stock still, waiting for the rest of the team to join her and her handler.

'He's down on that ledge.' Lucy shone her torch down the side of a gully onto a lump perched on a narrow ledge above a sheer drop.

'Oh, great!' Jack brushed snow out of his eyes and breathed out heavily. 'Well, now we've got a problem. That ledge is too bloody narrow to take a chicken, let alone one of us. OK, let's think this one through.'

They argued the options for a few minutes and then one of the team hurried over, his face anxious.

'We've managed to talk to him, but he's threatening to jump if we try and rescue him. He says he just wants to be left to die.'

Jack closed his eyes and muttered something unprintable. 'Oh, great. This I really need. Right, then, we need the doc.'

'I'm here.' Ally slipped off her rucksack and huddled deeper inside her coat. It was freezing. The darkness and bitter cold seemed to seep inside even the most sophisticated outdoor clothing. They had to get Geoff down the mountain fast or he'd die of hypothermia.

'Go with Ted and see if you can talk some sense into him,' Jack ordered, flashing his torch at the equipment officer. 'We'll prepare for the worst.'

Ally frowned. 'What's that?'

'Some poor sod having to rope up and go over the edge to

save him,' Jack said wryly, walking over to consult with his team.

Ally moved as close to the edge as was safe and called down, her words muffled by the falling snow. 'Geoff—it's me, Dr McGuire.'

For a moment there was no answer and she thought he couldn't have heard her, but just as she opened her mouth to shout again she heard his voice.

'I don't want to talk to you. I don't want to talk to anyone.'

'Geoff, please!' Ally lay down and wriggled closer to the edge. 'I just want to help.'

'No one can help.'

'For goodness' sake, someone get a rope on the woman before that cornice gives way!' Jack's voice drifted through the darkness and Ally shifted to allow them to secure a rope to her waist, her mind on Geoff rather than her own safety.

She thought fast, choosing her words carefully. 'Geoff—this isn't the way. Think of Mary!'

'I am thinking of Mary—that's why I'm doing this. She'd be better off without me.'

'That's not true.' Ally shivered slightly and wondered what state Geoff was in. If she was this cold then he must be freezing. 'She loves you so much.'

'Well, I don't deserve it.' Geoff huddled down, his outline barely visible in the darkness. 'Nothing I do ever turns out right. Look at me now! I tried to throw myself off the edge but I got caught on this stupid rock.'

Ally exchanged a look with Jack. 'Are you hurt, Geoff?'

'I don't care if I am!'

'Well, I care. I care a lot. I blame myself for this.'

There was a long silence. 'I don't know what you mean.'

'I should have seen how depressed you were.' Ally raised her voice above the wind. 'If you fall off that ledge, Geoff, I'll never be able to forgive myself.'

'Don't be stupid!' Geoff's words were barely audible.

'Let one of the boys come down and get you off there.'

'No!'

'Geoff, please!'

'I'll jump—I swear I'll jump.'

Ally closed her eyes and tried again. 'Me, then. Will you let me come down and talk? I know I can help you, Geoff, if you'll let me.'

There was another silence. 'OK. You. But no one else.'

'No!' Sean's voice was hoarse. 'Dammit, Jack, you can't let her go down there. It's too dangerous.'

Jack thought for a moment, indecision written clearly on his craggy features. Then he shrugged, his mind made up. 'I've got no choice, mate. She knows what she's doing and we'll have a tight hold on her.'

'No way!' Sean's eyes were black and furious and he stepped towards Jack menacingly. 'She's not going down there—'

'Oh, yes, I am.' Ally was already standing still while they fixed a harness around her hips and secured a rope.

'Now, you listen to me, girl!' Jack's jaw was rigid. 'You climb down and you assess him and you talk. You don't unclip the rope at any stage. You don't do anything heroic. Do you understand me?'

Ally nodded. 'Yes, but—'

Jack shook his head. 'No. No buts at all on this one. You don't unclip your own rope. We'll drop a spare rope for him and you can use that. Clear?'

'Yes, boss.' Ally gave a wry grin and moved towards the edge, but Sean grabbed her, his fingers closing like a vice on her arm.

'I'll go instead.'

'Don't be daft! You heard the man. He'll jump if you go.' Jack put a hand on Sean's arm and pulled him back, his voice gruff. 'You're not being rational, Sean. Think, man. Think.'

Sean stared at him for a long moment, his jaw tense, and then his eyes swivelled to Ally who was poised ready to go over the side.

'Right. Well, in that case, I want her roped to me.' He strode over to her, his eyes fierce. 'You do everything I say when I say it—do you hear me?'

She nodded mutely, wondering why she wasn't arguing with him. Despite the fact that her harness had been securely fitted and checked by one of the team, Sean checked it again, running his fingers along it and tugging until he gave a grunt of satisfaction. 'If he jumps, you let him go. Do you hear me?'

She stared at him. 'But—'

'Dammit, Ally, do you hear me?' He shook her slightly, his voice a deep growl of frustration. 'No heroics.'

'OK.' She nodded and wiped the snow out of her eyes. Aware of Jack standing slightly to one side, watching them both, she waited quietly while they checked and rechecked and made the final preparations. Geoff had gone over the side of a deep gully but the jagged, rocky sides made it unsuitable for abseiling. She was going to have to scramble down to him and join him on the ledge. Squinting down into the snowy darkness, she felt a moment of panic. Was there even room for two people on that ledge?

Taking a deep breath, she walked gingerly towards the edge and went over the side, using her hands and feet to feel for a way down, relying on Sean who was shouting instructions from above her.

It felt like for ever but finally her feet found the ledge and she flattened herself against the side of the gully to try and protect herself from the elements. The wind was rising, and without doubt the ledge was the most exposed place she'd ever been in her life.

'Geoff?'

He was huddled next to her, and with the light from the torch on her helmet she registered that there was no room for manoeuvre at all. The ledge was just too narrow. How on earth had he managed to fall onto it? By rights he should have been lying in a mangled heap at the bottom of the mountain.

'Geoff?' Was he unconscious? Certainly he wasn't moving

at all, and gingerly she crouched down next to him, feeling a rush of relief when he lifted his head, his ravaged features visible by her torchlight.

'Leave me alone. I don't know why you're risking your neck for me. You should have just let me die.'

'You're not going to die, Geoff.' Ally was finding it almost impossible to manoeuvre on the ledge with a rope attached to her waist, but she knew better than to risk removing it. 'First things first. Are you hurt anywhere?'

Geoff was silent for a moment then he shifted with a grunt. 'My ankle. I can't stand on it.'

'Right.' Ally slipped her gloved fingers into a handhold as the wind gusted against them. 'Well, let's get you to safety and then look at it. Will you let me put a harness on you?'

'No!' Geoff straightened and winced as his injured ankle took his weight. 'Dammit, I don't want to be rescued.'

'Geoff, nothing is ever this bad!' She was yelling now, her voice deadened by the wind. 'We can make it better. You've already beaten the alcohol.'

'Mary's better off without me.'

Ally thought for a moment and decided to use a different tack. 'Geoff Thompson, don't you dare pretend you care about Mary!'

He stared at her, bemused. 'Of course I care about Mary. That's why I'm doing this—so she doesn't have to be shackled to a loser any more.'

'If you cared about Mary you'd be thinking of her now. How do you think she feels, Geoff? She's been worried sick about you since you disappeared without letting anyone know where you were going. Then she gets a report that you've been sighted up here.' Ally flinched as the wind buffeted her against the rock, bruising her arm. 'She thinks you're already dead, Geoff, and she's beside herself. She adores you and she blames herself for not helping you.'

Geoff stared at her, his face anguished. 'She did help me. It wasn't her fault—'

'Well, she thinks it is!' Ally knew she was being brutal but gentle kindness hadn't worked at all. 'If you die now you'll be leaving Mary with a lifetime of grief and guilt. Is that what you want?'

Geoff shook his head slowly and groaned. 'No, it isn't. Of course it isn't what I want.'

'Then let me get you up this rockface to safety and then we can sort the whole thing out.'

He stared at her and then sagged, all the fight gone. 'All right. All right.'

Ally felt a rush of relief and fumbled with the spare harness on her waist. Unclipping it, she stepped towards Geoff, helping him into it and clipping it into place, checking it was secure before attaching the spare rope and yelling up to Jack.

'He's roped up. We need help to get him up—he's fractured his ankle.'

Jack's words were lost in the howling of wind that followed, and with a cry of alarm Ally lost her footing and went over the edge. Supported by the rope, she swung like a pendulum against the rockface and then the world went black.

'Ally? Ally, for God's sake!' The voice was male, urgent and very, very familiar.

Feeling as though an elephant were sitting on her eyelids, she opened her eyes briefly and closed them again as pain ripped through her head.

'She's awake, thank God!' That was Jack's voice, unusually strained. 'OK, let's get her off this mountain.'

'We're not moving her until I've checked her thoroughly.'

This time Ally's eyes flew open and clashed with Sean's.

'Tell me your name.' His voice was like a pistol crack and she blinked slowly.

'Minnie Mouse.' Her poor attempt at a joke fell on stony ground and he muttered under his breath.

'Ally, don't do this to me!'

Her smiled faltered as she saw the anguish in his dark eyes. He seemed to be hanging onto control by a thread.

'Sean, I'm OK. Really.' She saw the stubborn look on his face and sighed. 'OK, my name's Ally McGuire, I'm twenty-eight, I have a little girl called Charlie and—'

He frowned as he checked her pupillary reaction. 'And what?'

She swallowed. 'And I'm pregnant. Oh, Sean, what if I lose the baby?'

His jaw tensed. 'You won't lose it.'

'What's she worried about?' Jack came closer and frowned at them.

Sean opened his mouth but Ally shook her head. 'No! Nothing, Jack. How's Geoff?'

'Fine, thanks to you.' Jack waited for Sean to finish examining her and then secured her to the stretcher. 'Broken ankle and severe depression, but both those should heal with time. Lucy's with him. Do you want to supervise what they do with him, Sean?'

'No.' Sean shook his head, his eyes on Ally. 'I'm staying here.'

'But I'll…' Jack glanced at the lines of tension on his face and nodded slowly. 'On second thoughts, don't worry about it. I'll sort Geoff out. No problem.'

Ally watched Sean as he gave instructions to the rest of the mountain rescue team, tears suddenly clogging in her throat. She loved him so much. He was so strong and dependable and yet such a large part of him was locked away. And she didn't have the key.

'Are you in pain?' In seconds Sean was crouched down beside her, his eyes searching hers.

'No.' She closed her eyes but tears carried on seeping out from under her lashes. 'No, I'm fine.'

'Ally, for God's sake, talk to me!' Sean cupped her face with his hands and forced her to look at him. 'Why are you crying? Are you hurt?'

Yes. But not from her fall. She stared up at him. 'I'm sorry.'

'Sorry?' He frowned. 'Sorry for what?'

'For getting pregnant. I wasn't trying to trap you.'

His jaw clenched and he brushed away her tears with his thumb, a strange look in his eyes. 'Don't think about that now. We'll talk later.'

She had to let him know that it wasn't his responsibility. 'I don't want to marry you, Sean. You can relax.'

He didn't look relaxed. Far from it. In fact, if anything he seemed tenser than ever, his gaze a mixture of anger and frustration as he scowled at Jack. 'Are we ready? We need to get her down.'

Nobody spoke much as they made their way down the mountain. They were all too busy concentrating on the path in the darkness and foul weather, and all the way Ally was conscious of Sean right next to her. And he stayed right next to her until she was wheeled into a cubicle in the A and E department.

The consultant, Malcolm Roberts, strode in, and Sean gave him a brief nod, reporting Ally's condition succinctly and watching like a hawk while she was examined.

The consultant questioned her carefully and frowned at the cut on her head. 'I'll get someone to stitch that for you.'

Sean tensed. 'I'll do it.'

The consultant took one look at Sean's face and nodded. 'Fine. I'll get a nurse to help you.'

'I want to take her home tonight.'

Malcolm glanced up from the notes he was writing. 'Will someone be with her?'

Sean was looking at Ally, his expression unreadable. 'I'll be with her.'

'In that case, I don't see why not.' The consultant carried on writing and then slipped the pen back into his breast pocket. 'You know what to look for. Any worries, just bring her back.'

'One other thing.' Sean cleared his throat, his eyes still on Ally. 'She's pregnant. She's had no lower abdominal pain but I'd like her scanned.'

Malcolm paused and then nodded. 'No problem. I'll ring the labour ward and arrange it for you.'

Ally lay still during the scan, not daring to look at Sean. She'd expected him to make his excuses when it had come to the undeniable evidence of their child, but he'd stayed firmly by her side while she'd been wheeled into a side ward on her own, and was standing out of her line of vision. Was he watching?

'It all looks fine.' The ultrasonographer smiled at her and wiped the jelly from Ally's abdomen. 'No worries there. He's well protected at the moment so it's unlikely he came to any harm.'

'Thanks.' Ally gave her a shaky smile and watched her leave the room, feeling suddenly awkward to be alone with Sean. 'I'd better get dressed.'

'No, wait!' He raked long fingers through his cropped hair, looking thoroughly agitated and very, very male. 'Dammit, Ally, we need to talk and I don't think I can wait until we get home.'

Her hands clenched. She wasn't up to this. Later, maybe she'd be able to pretend she could cope with losing him, but not at the moment when she felt so vulnerable and he was being so protective.

'Sean, I really can't—not now...'

'I just want you to listen, that's all.' He took a deep breath and sat down on the edge of the bed, prising her hands apart and taking them in his. 'This has, without any doubt, been the worst day of my life.'

Her heart stopped and her voice was little more than a whisper. 'You mean, seeing the baby?'

'Dammit, no!' His voice was raw with emotion and he dropped her hands and rubbed his temples with long fingers. 'I don't mean that at all! Seeing the baby was—well, it was incredible.'

He stood up abruptly and walked over to the window, turning his back on her so that she couldn't see the expression on his face. 'I don't know where to start. I wasn't going to say any of this until we got home but I don't think I can wait that long.'

Her heart was thudding in slow motion. 'Say what?'

There was a long silence. 'I've never let myself trust anyone. I suppose in a way I was trying to test what the social worker told me.'

Ally fixed her eyes on those broad shoulders which were still shutting her out. 'And what was that?'

'That I was difficult. I was a difficult baby, a difficult toddler and a difficult teenager. My mother couldn't cope and so she gave me away. I wasn't the dream baby she'd imagined—'

'Sean—'

'I was passed from foster-family to foster-family and all the time I grew more difficult. Whenever I went somewhere new I pushed them to the limit. Testing them. Trying to find a family who'd love me unconditionally, I suppose. It didn't take me long to start believing that that kind of love didn't exist outside fairy stories. Not for me, anyway.'

Ally felt scalding tears fill her eyes. 'Oh, Sean—'

'I've never been any good at relationships but I know I don't need to tell you that.' He stared out of the window, his voice flat and expressionless. 'All through my childhood, whenever I started to feel affection for someone I was moved on. You've no idea what that does to a child—feeling unwanted. Unloved. In the end I told myself I didn't need it and developed a defence mechanism. The only person I relied on was myself. I never allowed myself to love anyone in case I lost them.'

'Please, come here, Sean.'

His shoulders stiffened but he still didn't look at her. 'When I grew up I just kept the same pattern. I never allowed myself to love anyone because I couldn't bear the thought of what would happen if it didn't last. So I was always the one in control. The one who ended the relationship. And I'd come across so many miserable kids from broken homes in my time in care that I resolved never to risk having a child of my own in case the relationship went wrong.

'And then I met you.' He turned slowly and his eyes clung to hers, all the pain of his traumatic youth revealed in those dark depths. 'You were everything I'd ever dreamed of. Strong, gentle, clever, feminine, shy, sexy—so many things all in one package. I wanted you badly.'

Her blue eyes were soft. 'I wanted you, too.'

'That night when we made love—' He broke off and stared out of the window again, his eyes distant, remembering. 'You were so warm and giving and innocent, and I felt as though I never wanted to let you go. All I wanted to do was hold you and protect you. I've never felt like that about another person before.'

'And you panicked.'

He turned his head to look at her, a wry smile playing around his hard mouth. 'Panic barely begins to describe it. Suddenly I felt vulnerable, and I'm not used to feeling like that.'

Ally felt a sudden rush of love and sympathy. It was taking so much courage for him to admit these feelings, feelings which he was used to keeping hidden deep inside himself.

'And then you found out I was pregnant.'

'Yes.' His jaw clenched but his eyes held hers. 'I felt as though the ground had shifted underneath me. As if everything I'd ever believed in had collapsed. I couldn't believe I'd been so careless.'

'It wasn't your fault.'

His mouth twisted. 'Of course it was my fault. I'd virtually seduced you—tempted you and teased you until you'd wanted me, too. If I had been so bothered I would have questioned you more closely, but the truth was I was so desperate for you that it wouldn't have made any difference what you'd said to me.'

'You didn't seduce me.'

He gave a wry smile. 'You were a virgin, Ally.'

'I still knew what I was doing.'

'Maybe. I don't know.' He shrugged and glanced out of the window again, fighting for control. 'Either way, you were pregnant and I was suddenly forced to confront all those feelings I'd ducked all my life.'

'You don't have to—'

'Dammit, Ally, stop saying that!' He slammed his fist against the wall and glared at her. 'Of course I have to! It's my baby, too.'

'But you don't want it.'

'I do want it. I don't want this baby growing up, not knowing its father.'

His eyes burned into hers and she felt her heart tear into two. How could she stand it? Seeing him occasionally with their child but not having him for herself? How would she ever get over him if he was constantly re-entering her life? It would be the worst possible torture but she couldn't deny him his rights, either for his sake or that of their child.

With a huge effort she managed what she hoped was a reassuring smile. 'I'd never stop you seeing your child, Sean. I'm not like that.'

He contemplated her in silence, a muscle flickering in his hard jaw. 'I'm not talking about visitation rights, Ally.'

Her cheeks blanched. He couldn't mean— She sat bolt upright. 'You wouldn't take my baby away from me?'

'Take your...?' He blinked several times, his expression stunned. 'For God's sake, Ally, what type of man do you take me for?'

She swallowed and sank back against the pillows, relief swamping her. 'I—'

'On second thoughts, don't answer that question.' He gave a wry, self-deprecating smile and sat down on the covers next to her, lifting her hands in his and holding them tightly. 'I haven't done much to earn your good opinion, have I? First I pursue you relentlessly, then I seduce you, then I tell you I don't want commitment, and then I round it all off by accusing you of trying to trap me by getting pregnant. It's no wonder you won't marry me.'

'Sean, I—'

'No, let me finish.' He cleared his throat and his fingers tightened painfully on hers. 'I know you think I'm not capable of commitment but you're wrong. I never knew how I felt about you until I saw you go down onto that ledge. I thought I was going to go mad with worry. All I kept thinking was that I never should have allowed it, and if anything happened to you I'd have lost everything.'

What was he saying? 'Sean—'

'You said you loved me Ally.' His voice was hoarse. 'Did you mean it?'

She swallowed hard. 'Of course I meant it.'

'Well, I love you, too.' He dropped her hands and cupped her face, forcing her to look at him. 'I've never said that to another human being in my life before. I've never allowed myself to love anyone before, but with you it wasn't something I could control. It just happened. You were right when you said that I never take risks. I don't, usually. Not emotional ones, anyway, but with you I had no choice. I realised that today.'

Tears slid down her cheeks and she blinked them away. 'You love me?'

He gave her a lopsided grin. 'Madly.'

She sniffed. 'You want to marry me?'

The grin widened and he nodded. 'I'm going to marry you whether you like it or not. Someone has to stop you taking stupid risks.'

She wiped her eyes on her sleeve. 'I can't believe you mean it. I keep thinking I've trapped you.'

'You have.' His mouth hovered tantalisingly close to hers, the look in his eyes turning her legs to jelly. 'I'm well and truly trapped. Just don't ever let me go.'

'Never.' Ally shook her head, her heart thudding in slow motion. 'I love you.'

'I know you do.' His eyes softened and his lips brushed hers, his expression wicked. 'And I'm going to make you prove it—over and over again.'

Part of her was still anxious. 'But you've never settled in one place…'

'Well, I certainly can't see myself permanently in a GP practice, you're right about that.' He gave her a rueful smile. 'Rumour has it that Malcolm Roberts is leaving for pastures new, so there's a vacancy for an A and E consultant coming up.'

Her face brightened. 'That would be perfect.'

'No.' His eyes were suddenly serious, his knuckles brushing her cheek in a gesture of such gentle affection that she felt her breathing stop. 'It's marrying you that would be perfect. You do realise you haven't given me an answer yet.'

'Haven't I?' Swamped by happiness, her eyes teased him and she slid her arms round his neck to pull him closer again.

'Well, Dr McGuire?' He buried his face in her soft hair and gave a groan. 'Are you willing to take a chance on me?'

'Well, Dr Nicholson, let me think—' Ally gasped as he cupped her face in his hands and kissed her gently. 'The answer is yes. I happen to think you're worth the risk.'

MILLS & BOON®
Makes any time special™

Mills & Boon publish 29 new titles every month. Select from...

Modern Romance™   Tender Romance™

Sensual Romance™

Medical Romance™   Historical Romance™

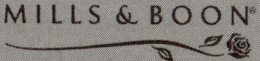

Medical Romance™

A MOTHER BY NATURE by Caroline Anderson
Audley Memorial Hospital

Adam Bradbury is a gifted paediatrician and a devoted father. But he is sure that his inability to have children of his own will push any woman away. But Anna knows that Adam is wrong and she is determined to prove it...

HEART'S COMMAND by Meredith Webber

Major Harry Graham had been drafted in to save the outback town of Murrawarra from torrential flood water but he hadn't bargained on Dr Kirsten McPherson's refusal to be evacuated...

A VERY SPECIAL CHILD by Jennifer Taylor
Dalverston General Hospital

Nurse Laura Grady knew that her special needs son, Robbie, would always be the centre of her life. Could paediatric registrar Mark Dawson persuade her that he wanted both of them to be the centre of his?

On sale 2nd February 2001

Available at most branches of WH Smith, Tesco, Martins, Borders, Easons, Volume One/James Thin and most good paperback bookshops

MILLS & BOON®

Medical Romance™

THE ELUSIVE DOCTOR by Abigail Gordon

Ambitious Dr Nina Lombard did not want to be in the quaint village of Stepping Dearsley! But now that she was working for Dr Robert Carslake, Nina found that she had a reason to stay...

A SURGEON'S REPUTATION by Lucy Clark

Dr James Crosby has made his attraction clear to Dr Holly Mayberry but something from his past is holding him back. When James's reputation is put on the line Holly knows she has a chance to win his trust and his heart...

DELIVERING LOVE by Fiona McArthur

New Author

Poppy McCrae has always used complementary therapies in her work as a midwife. Paediatrician Jake Sheppard thoroughly disapproves of her methods. Can Poppy persuade Jake to accept her and her beliefs?

On sale 2nd February 2001

Available at most branches of WH Smith, Tesco, Martins, Borders, Easons, Volume One/James Thin and most good paperback bookshops

MILLS & BOON

THIS TIME...
MARRIAGE

Three brides get the chance to make it This Time... Forever.

**Great value—
3 compelling novels in 1.**

Available from 2nd February 2001

4 FREE books and a surprise gift!

We would like to take this opportunity to thank you for reading this Mills & Boon® book by offering you the chance to take FOUR more specially selected titles from the Medical Romance™ series absolutely FREE! We're also making this offer to introduce you to the benefits of the Reader Service™—

- ★ FREE home delivery
- ★ FREE gifts and competitions
- ★ FREE monthly Newsletter
- ★ Exclusive Reader Service discounts
- ★ Books available before they're in the shops

Accepting these FREE books and gift places you under no obligation to buy, you may cancel at any time, even after receiving your free shipment. Simply complete your details below and return the entire page to the address below. *You don't even need a stamp!*

YES! Please send me 4 free Medical Romance books and a surprise gift. I understand that unless you hear from me, I will receive 6 superb new titles every month for just £2.40 each, postage and packing free. I am under no obligation to purchase any books and may cancel my subscription at any time. The free books and gift will be mine to keep in any case.

M1ZEA

Ms/Mrs/Miss/Mr ....Initials.....................................
BLOCK CAPITALS PLEASE

Surname ....

Address ....

....

....Postcode...............................

Send this whole page to:
UK: FREEPOST CN81, Croydon, CR9 3WZ
EIRE: PO Box 4546, Kilcock, County Kildare (stamp required)

Offer valid in UK and Eire only and not available to current Reader Service subscribers to this series. We reserve the right to refuse an application and applicants must be aged 18 years or over. Only one application per household. Terms and prices subject to change without notice. Offer expires 31st July 2001. As a result of this application, you may receive further offers from Harlequin Mills & Boon and other carefully selected companies. If you would prefer not to share in this opportunity please write to The Data Manager at the address above.

Mills & Boon® is a registered trademark owned by Harlequin Mills & Boon Limited.
Medical Romance™ is being used as a trademark.